Veronica Bennett works part time as an English lecturer. She began her writing career as a freelance journalist, but soon moved into fiction. She is the author of *The Boy-free Zone*, *Fish Feet*, *Monkey* and, for younger readers, *Dandelion and Bobcat*. The seed for *Angelmonster* was planted when Veronica happened to see a portrait of Mary Shelley hanging in the National Portrait Gallery. "The look in her eyes fascinated me," says Veronica. "It came to me that history and biography can tell us facts and speculate on her feelings – but only a novel can bend history to the power of the imagination and explore what might have been behind those eyes." Researching Mary's story, Veronica was struck by "what happened to her at such a young age, and at a period of history when, we are led to suppose, young girls were prevented from doing anything." Veronica has lived in Israel, Spain and Canada, and now lives in Middlesex with her family.

Books by the same author

The Boy-free Zone
Dandelion and Bobcat
Fish Feet
Monkey

ANGELMONSTER

VERONICA BENNETT

WALKER BOOKS
AND SUBSIDIARIES
LONDON · BOSTON · SYDNEY · AUCKLAND

First published 2005 by Walker Books Ltd
87 Vauxhall Walk, London SE11 5HJ

2 4 6 8 10 9 7 5 3

Text © 2005 Veronica Bennett
Cover illustration © 2005 Jeff Fisher

The right of Veronica Bennett to be identified as author of this work has been
asserted by her in accordance with the Copyright, Designs and Patents Act 1988

This book has been typeset in M Bembo and Stuyvesant ICG

Printed and bound in Great Britain by Bookmarque Ltd, Croydon, Surrey

British Library Cataloguing in Publication Data:
a catalogue record for this book
is available from the British Library

ISBN 0-7445-5986-3

www.walkerbooks.co.uk

To my father

Blood and Water

*J*ane was crying. She snorted and sniffed, unable to wipe away the tears because both her hands were entangled in my corset-strings. The thin, unbreakable strings had sliced through the tender skin of her finger joints. Her blood was staining them reddish-brown.

"What will Papa say?" she wailed.

"Pull harder, you donkey!"

The corset was crushing my ribcage. I kicked my step-sister's ankle. She pulled harder. Breathless, I nodded encouragement. A curl paper fell out of my hair and fluttered to the carpet.

Controlling her tears, Jane stood back. "There." She paused to sniff. "But Papa will be so angry! I cannot imagine what he will say."

"Well, *I* can." It was hard to breathe under such restriction, but I thickened my voice and wrinkled my eyebrows in imitation of my father. "'My dear child, anyone who inflicts such violence on their person is truly fashion's slave. You are a prisoner of vanity. I am much aggrieved.'"

I turned this way and that, admiring the effect of the corset on my body. My stomach was so flat it was almost concave. The whalebone had pushed my breasts, which were not very significant under ordinary circumstances, onto a sort of plateau, where they lay like jelly arranged on a plate.

"Do not forget," I reminded Jane, "I am quite safe from public disgrace, since Papa cannot say anything in front of his guests."

She had almost stopped crying, and was wiping her nose. "Why not?"

"Because, you innocent thing, he is a *Radical*." Hoping to amuse her, I struck a pose like a Greek goddess carrying an invisible urn on her head. "A new thinker, a philosopher unrivalled by the ancients. How can he *possibly* be considered old-fashioned?"

"Oh, stuff." Jane sucked her bloodied fingers wearily. "Your clever talk fails to impress me. You know you will have to endure Mama's scolding, and I will have to defend you, as usual."

"Jane…" Impatiently I turned round. As we faced each other in the candlelight Jane's troubled face looked like a yellow, shadowed moon. "Jane, dear, think of it as a *game*. Play-acting, a treasure hunt, what you will. Now, do you want to join in or not?"

My stepsister's fanciful nature was never oppressed for long. She dropped a maid's curtsy, her finger in the corner of her mouth. "Yes, Miss Mary. If you please, miss, what are my orders?"

I spoke in my lightest, most elegant voice – the voice I would use during the drawing-room farce which awaited us downstairs. "Watch me and do as I do. Flirt. Laugh at all their jokes. Allow your profile to be seen in silhouette, with the firelight behind you, but protect your face from its heat with your fan. Make sure your stockings are showing when you sit down." I turned back to the mirror. "If Papa insists on the attendance of his daughters at this infernal gathering of lechers and pontificators –"

"Only *two* of his daughters," interrupted Jane. "Fanny is not expected."

"Fanny does not count. But if you and I must be shown off like circus freaks, the least we can do is have some sport with the gentlemen, if that is what they are."

Jane and I were both sixteen. As I watched her widen her innocent, already wide eyes, I reflected that no one, whatever they might say about my own appearance, would ever include innocence in the description. My face was thin, with a rather more obvious nose than I would have liked. When people noticed my eyes it was not only to admire them, though I well knew how beautiful they were, but also to comment on the maturity of their expression. *Born knowing*, I had once overheard a lady guest say when I was a ten-year-old being paraded as after-supper entertainment. *She will make her mark, that child.*

"Poor Fanny," observed Jane, with mischief, not sympathy, in her voice. "She is to have no sport!"

Her curls bobbed around her smooth, well-made face. She and her brother Charles had the kind of luxurious good looks that people remarked on with admiration, much to Jane's satisfaction. But a consolation to my own vanity was Fanny, my half-sister. When my father had married my mother, he had taken in her little daughter Fanny and treated the child as his own. But after our mother had died giving birth to me, and Papa had married the mother of Jane and Charles, Fanny began to seem like an outsider, with little connection to anyone else in the house. Quieter than Jane and me, with a melancholy disposition, her inelegantly arranged features provided me with a daily reminder of my own good fortune. My loyalty to my half-sister was secure, but a shared mother could not make me admire Fanny's looks the way I admired Jane's.

"Jane, you really should try to find some affection in your heart for Fanny," I told her. "Now fetch my gown. Without getting blood on it, if you please."

Jane and I had been stepsisters so long that neither of us could remember a time without the other. But the bond between us was based more on familiarity than on spontaneous feeling. Indeed, I sometimes wondered if I was capable of true love for either of my sisters. Perhaps it is not possible for sisters who are competitors for the attention of a beloved father to find any attention left over for each other. And however close Jane and I were, I could never forgive her mother for her invasion of the place in Papa's heart which my own clever, sad mama had occupied.

The gown Jane held out was made of white muslin. It had an underskirt, also of muslin, decorated at the bottom, where it showed under the gown, with a simple scrolling of looped ribbon hastily sewn on by Fanny, the only needle-woman among us, the previous afternoon. Its sleeves were short, barely covering my shoulders. My bosom nestled in the deeply cut, high-waisted bodice as if it had been fashioned by a master sculptor.

I looked at my reflection. Charming. Desirable. Even

with my hair, bright as silk, still in papers.

"And now, Jane – the bucket."

"Oh…" she began uncertainly.

"*Now*, or the water will be cold!"

She lifted the bucket of water which stood in the corner. It was heavy. "My fingers hurt," she complained, hauling the bucket across the room to where I stood barefoot in the largest basin we had been able to smuggle out of the kitchen.

"I don't care a straw about your fingers or any other part of your ignorant carcass," I told her. "Go on, do it. I am ready."

I put my hands over my hair and closed my eyes tightly, bracing myself. Huffing and puffing, Jane stood on a chair. As she tipped the bucket, the water ran over my shoulders and down my back and chest and legs, splashing into the basin. Gasping, stifling screams behind my clenched teeth, I bore the soaking. I did not want my stepmother, who had not yet discovered that we had sent the maid away and locked the door, bustling towards the source of the noise.

The looking-glass reflected exactly what I wanted to see. The soaked gown clung to my body like skin. Better still, it had made both the dress and the chemise I wore under the corset almost transparent. Grinning with satisfaction, I picked up my fan and spread it. "Quick, my hair. I must get downstairs before the gown dries. Quick, quick!"

Her fingers trembling, Jane began to take the papers out of my hair. "Lord, how you shiver! And the drawing-room is so draughty. What can you be thinking of?"

"I am thinking of my father's favour," I told her truthfully. "Making him attend to *me*, not to … anyone else." I could not admit that I meant her unlovable mother. "And if a wet dress is good enough for the ladies of the French court, it is good enough for me."

"There!" Jane let the last curl spring back from her finger. She looked at me over her fan. She was at her most appealing, in her evening dress with the light falling on her jewellery and her jewel-like dark eyes. "Oh, Mary, have you considered that tonight might be ... you know ... the night?" she asked in a rapturous whisper. "The night when we find the love of a true gentleman, who desires us above all others, and is prepared to declare his passion?"

"If so, he had better be of a strong constitution," I declared, picking up my train. "Our passion may well be greater than his!"

"Perhaps he will be a poet," she suggested, taking my arm. "And you know how passionate *they* are."

"To be sure," I agreed, "a poet is the only acceptable sort of lover these days."

Jane and I had often discussed the possibility of falling in love with a poet. If poetry was any measure of a man, we had observed, everything we longed for in a lover – romance, desire, spirit, soul – was clearly contained in it.

Excited but wary, we stepped onto the landing. Jane gripped my arm with more force. "Oh, Mary!" she breathed. "If only a poet could fall in love with me, or even *you!*"

Frivolous words, but prophetic ones. And prophetic words revisit us, in and out of our dreams.

Riches and Ruin

$\mathcal{M}$y father was not rich or noble, but he was an influential writer, and so had my mother been. Although I was only sixteen, I was determined to follow the ideals of freedom set out in my parents' work. Freedom for women! Freedom for slaves! Freedom from marriage! These things seemed to me right and joyous and true, and from the moment I had been old enough to understand them I had resolved to adopt them as principles for my own life.

It was scarcely credible, then, that my dear father could have taken for his second wife a woman so different in her outlook.

"It's disgusting," said my stepmother peevishly. "Respectable young women do not display themselves in public half naked."

She and Jane and I were in the drawing-room, after the guests had gone. My father, who considered the chastisement of daughters women's work, had retired to bed. I was tired and miserable: tonight had *not* been "the night". My prediction of a roomful of lechers and pontificators had proved uncomfortably accurate, and the wet dress had proved uncomfortably cold. I was silent.

"A *wet* dress!" she persisted. "Do you think you are the Emperor's mistress? Or an actress? Or – may God forgive me – something lower even than an actress, that you shame your family so? That *corset*, Mary!"

Low though my spirits were, I rushed to defend myself. "Mama, it is precisely *because* I am young, and respectable, that I can wear the height of fashion. I want people to notice me. Are you not forever reminding Jane and me that we must attract rich husbands since Papa can give us no fortune? But I want some gaiety in my life before I am married."

"Gaiety! Then it was merely to amuse yourself that you embarrassed your father, shamed me, set the servants tittle-tattling and—"

"Enchanted the entire room?"

She was silenced. The three of us sat there, not quite glaring at each other, while she collected herself. It did not take long.

"It is true that you must marry men with money," she said. The flesh on her neck quivered as she spoke. She had been as attractive as Jane when she was young, but had turned into a too-ample middle-aged woman, with rouged cheeks and girlish clothes. "But you will not attract wealth if you behave like a harlot. Respectable men want respectable wives!"

Jane could no longer contain herself. Secure of her position as the indulged daughter of a vain woman, she was even more careless of her mother's authority than I.

"Why should we care about wealth?" she asked. "Is not a gentleman a gentleman because of his qualities, even if he has no fortune? Might we not earn our own living, as men do?"

Her mother shook her head in vexation. "Jane, I will not have you repeating these dangerous ideas. Earn your own living? Piffle!"

Under the table, Jane pressed my foot with hers. The message meant, "Go on, Mary, deliver the final blow".

"But, Mama," I said sweetly, "surely these are principles which Papa himself believes in?"

Mama was annoyed, but powerless. She opened the fan she had been twisting in her hands and shut it again with a whipcrack. "You do not understand what you are saying, child," she said to Jane. Then she turned her small eyes, as dark as Jane's but devoid of innocence, on me. "And as for you, my pretty miss, you had better remember that no good ever came of impertinence."

I did not reply. Neither did I lower my eyes. I looked at her fearlessly, my heart gripped by dislike so profound it gave me courage.

"I expect more ladylike conduct in future," she continued. "I do not expect to be embarrassed by a young person in whose upbringing I have invested such unstinting effort. If you end in ruin, you silly girl, it will be by your own hand. And you will *not* take my daughter down with you."

I awoke in darkness. I was screaming. Unaware of the darkness, unaware of my surroundings, unaware of myself, still in my dream, I sat up, rocking an invisible baby in my arms. "Mama! Mama! Dear God, I have killed her!" Jane was there. She must have left her own bed when she heard my cries. I could feel her beside me, a shawl flung over her nightdress, her hands searching in the dark, her voice whispering.

"It's only a dream, Mary dear. Let me stay with you until you go back to sleep."

Taking me by the shoulders, she lowered me to the pillow and climbed into the bed beside me. I swallowed the next scream, shivering in the warm bed, my body tense, my brain active with silent words I had not the breath to utter. Mama, Mama ... forgive me. Because I was born you died. But I never meant to be born, or for you to die. What manner of ungodly baby kills its own creator? A vile, pitiless creature, with no regard for life's beauty or meaning. A monster-baby. A freak.

I listened to the rhythm of Jane's breathing. My nightmares had become routine to her. Now that she had silenced me, and the rest of the household could resume their slumbers, she would soon be asleep. I found her hand and tightened my fingers around hers.

"Mama, forgive me," I said silently. "Your earthly nightmares were real enough, but now you are free of them. Will I ever be set free, and allowed to sleep in peace?"

Second-best Blue Silk

$\mathcal{O}$ur family business was a bookshop. It stood in a row of other shops, in a part of London which Papa said was good for business because it was always crowded. But it was noisy and dirty too. We lived above the shop, our drawing-room window overlooking the street. Mama's sofa, strewn with cushions which Fanny had embroidered with peacocks, was positioned by the window so she could see who came and went while screened from view by lace curtains.

Neither Jane nor I, nor Fanny, were allowed to sit on Mama's sofa, but we preferred the window-seat anyway. It was just big enough for two children or very young girls. I used to sit there for hours, writing and reading and dreaming, while Mama was about her housekeeping business, or unwell and keeping to her room, or out paying calls and gossiping about her wayward daughters. Her dear Fanny was the only sensible one, she would declare. Jane and I were "miss-ish", she had decided. Our heads were full of "notions", as she called them.

Notions they may have been, but I preferred to think of

whatever was in my own head as dreams. I dreamed of travelling, far beyond the confines of London and England, to the other side of the world. I dreamed about heroes and heroines of stories I had read, and imagined my own hero. Often I wrote stories of my own. My first effort, written to amuse Jane when we were nine years old, was the tale of a maiden whose foolishness led to her being eaten by a bear. Later I began several romantic novels, influenced greatly by those of more experienced authors. But I did not show them to anyone except Papa, who, being a writer himself, understood the desire for self-expression that burned within his daughter.

"Your dear mother would have been happy to see you take up the pen, Mary," he told me. "And, I must confess, so am I."

Aside from my writing about bears or betrayals, Jane and I wrote down our dreams. Do all girls do this when they are growing up? Jane and I turned it into a game. We would each take a piece of paper from Mama's writing desk and write at the top, "The man I marry will…" Then a good many silent minutes would pass while we made our lists, sharing the inkstand like good girls working for their governess. Not that we ever had a governess.

Jane and I knew there was a world beyond marriage. It was the world envisaged by my mother when she had written about women's freedom. But we also knew that marriage was the only means by which we could escape from the narrow house above the bookshop and truly begin to live.

My list always began with "swear utter fidelity". I liked to picture whoever-he-was kneeling before me, his hand on the breast of his fashionable coat, bowing low enough for me to inspect the elegance of his long, curly hair, telling me in a breaking voice that he had forsaken all others and wanted only me. Me, me, *me,* for ever.

Jane's beginnings varied. She liked "buy me a great house in the country, where I can give parties and eat ice cream" when she was younger, but by the time she was fifteen this had changed to either "adore babies" or "keep a carriage and six".

Further down my own list came "be clever", though I was vague as to how this cleverness would show itself. A banker, or a lawyer? A mine or factory owner? A publisher? Journalist? Or a political philosopher like Papa, thinking, writing, being toasted at dinners and celebrated in society? A musician or a painter, sought by every salon hostess in London? Perhaps even … no, a romantic poet was merely a joke between Jane and myself.

The shop was dark and low-ceilinged. The day after my wet dress escapade, when I had been instructed by my loving mama not to venture outside as I would catch my death, I sought my father there.

"Papa, I am so bored upstairs," I pleaded. "Mama will not let me go out."

"Quite right."

He emerged from between the bookshelves with a pile of books, smiling his serious smile. The sharp nose I had inherited looked sharper than usual. "But since you are here, you may make yourself useful. If you please, my dear, would you put these back on the top shelf? You are more agile than I."

"Of course, Papa."

He hesitated before he gave me the books. "And about last night's performance…"

"You forgive me, do you not, Papa?"

He nodded, more with relief than condescension. "You are your mother's daughter, Mary, in more than name. A wild spirit. But I know you are a good girl."

I sighed. I *was* a good girl. I spent my entire time trying to please unpleasable people, it seemed. I took the books and, lifting the hem of my skirt, made a shaky ascent of the ladder. When the books were safely on the shelf I gathered the skirt around my knees and prepared to go down.

The bell on the door clanged as a customer came in. I stayed where I was, perched on the top rung of the ladder, obscured by the darkness. I often hid in the shadowy shop like this. I liked to watch my father being a Great Mind, encouraging those with money to part with it and those without to share as much philosophical discussion as time and idleness would allow.

I shifted my position to obtain a better view of the visitor. The light from the front window revealed a tall, slightly-built man, still wearing his hat. He was young, no more than twenty or so, with a blue jacket, tan breeches, a badly tied tie and an armful of books. He put the books down and said cheerfully to Papa, "Good afternoon, sir. What chance a sovereign for these?"

His voice was measured, yet at the same time urgent, as if the simple words had important meaning. Curiosity crept over me. Was this young man a regular customer, known to Papa?

My father began to inspect the books. While he did so, the young man removed his hat, leant on the door frame and gazed around the shop. I saw that his face was well shaped, with a high brow and clean-shaven chin. He had extraordinary eyes – large, and expressive even at a distance – and light, curly hair.

Curly hair!

I lifted my skirt a little higher. Happily I was wearing my second-best dress, a blue silk. It was fine stuff, trimmed with recently replaced lace. And my hair, washed for the party last night, had been curled again this morning. I looked as well as I ever *could* look.

"Papa!" I called boldly. "Would you hold the ladder? I fear it is a little unsteady."

The customer looked up when he heard my voice. "Er… Miss? If you please … may *I* assist you?"

Peering into the recesses of the shop, he located first my boots, then my stockings, then my skirt, then my face at the top of the ladder. He placed his foot sturdily on the bottom rung. His upturned face showed amusement, but no mockery. "My apologies," he said. "Are you this gentleman's daughter?"

I began, slowly, to descend. "Yes, sir."

My father could not allow himself to be excluded. He advanced and made a small bow. "She is my middle daughter, sir. Her name is—"

"Mary," interrupted the gentleman. "You see, I know it. By repute, all your daughters are charming."

Papa bowed lower. As I gained the lowest rung, and the young man had to remove his foot to make way for mine, I felt the blood rise to my face.

"I see repute is not mistaken," he said.

It was gallantry, but I was flattered. Although in my mother's philosophy women were equal with men, and curtsying was reserved for servants and sycophants, I performed a low curtsy. Very prettily, I thought.

The man bowed. "Shelley," he said.

"Mr Shelley is a poet, my dear," added my father proudly.

I could not prevent myself from blushing. The rules of flirtation I had recited to Jane last night deserted me. This man had been plucked from romantic fantasy and placed here before me. In the blue-coated figure I saw my dreams and excitement beyond any "sport" my sister and I had ever concocted. I managed to say "How do you do?", but so quietly he could not have heard.

"I believe I dined in your company some years ago, when you were a little girl," he said.

"Oh!" I exclaimed, raking my brain for the memory of this occasion. Suddenly it was there: pink ribbons in Jane's hair, flowers on the table, a young man laughing with my father and drinking a lot of wine. "Oh, was that *you*?"

"Mr Shelley will be a great poet one day," observed Papa.

"Sir, you flatter me," said Shelley, bowing.

As I watched him, another memory came to mind. A few weeks ago Papa had shown Mama something in the news-paper, shaking his finger at it excitedly and telling her that this poet, a man of his acquaintance, was on the verge of success. Jane and I had taken no notice. We had assumed that the poet, like the rest of Papa's acquaintance, would be middle-aged, tedious and less talented than he supposed.

Papa recollected that he was in the middle of a business transaction. He went to the desk. "I can offer you fifteen shillings, Mr Shelley."

"You are kind, sir, but eighteen would be the least I could accept."

"Sixteen shillings and sixpence."

Shelley nodded, replaced his hat and touched the brim in

my direction. He pocketed the coins gravely. "My thanks, sir. Good day."

The door clanged. Papa and I exchanged a look. Then the door clanged again.

"Will you allow me to call?" Shelley asked my father.

"Certainly."

He bowed, and was gone.

I no longer had to worry my father for useful employment. Hitching the second-best blue silk dress above my knees I bounded up the stairs two at a time, in a fashion long since banned by my stepmother, laughed at by Papa, imitated by Jane and disapproved of by Fanny. All the way up I called, "Jane! Jane!"

But it was Fanny who came out of the drawing-room, sewing in hand. "What are you doing?" she asked sharply. "Mama and I wondered what the noise could be."

Fanny was barely four years older than Jane and me, but she seemed ancient. Even Papa, with his habits of pursuing famous people and drinking more than was good for him, seemed younger. She was wearing an ill-fitting afternoon dress, and her hair was in its usual severe braids, with no softening curls at the temples such as Jane and I wore.

"Well?" she demanded.

"I am looking for Jane."

"You are always looking for Jane," said Fanny, and went back into the drawing-room. "She is in her room."

Climbing the next flight of stairs no less noisily, I opened Jane's door without knocking. "Guess who has just come into the shop!"

Jane was lying on her bed reading a novel. When I entered she put the book down, puckering her eyebrows.

"The King? The Duke of Wellington? Napoleon himself?"

"I am in earnest." I sat on the bed. "Do you remember when we were about twelve, a man coming to dinner whom Papa said was going to be a poet?"

Her eyes took on a faraway look. "Do you mean Mr Coleridge, who recited that dreadfully long poem about an albatross?"

"No, that was much longer ago. I was only six then, and you were asleep, and you only know the story of *The Ancient Mariner* because I told you afterwards, so do not show off, please. This is a Mr Shelley. Papa says he is an aristocrat – the son of an earl, or something, though he does not use his title. He came into the shop today and sold Papa some books, and spoke to me and said he remembered me."

Jane looked cynical. "And did he *buy* any books?"

"No, but what has that to do with it?"

"Have you never noticed how titled people are always the least ready to part with their money?"

"Jane!" I was exasperated. "Sometimes you sound more like your mama than is good for you!"

She smiled her beautiful smile. "I am teasing you because I am envious that you were there and I was not." She leant towards me. "*And* you were wearing that blue dress which I covet so shamelessly. What was he like?"

I took her by the shoulders. "Like a god. Like an angel. Like every hero in every romance you have ever read." Releasing her, I took up her book and looked at the title. "Like the most perfect example of male beauty represented in this book. Which, by the way, I have never heard of."

"Why, Mary, how old-fashioned you are!" Peevishly she

took it back. "It is newly published. Mama borrowed it from somebody."

"It must be a novel, then, since Mama reads nothing else."

"It *is* a novel." She sighed. "But so far it is rather dull. Three or four families in a country village, that is all."

"Abominable!" I put my hand to my throat, affecting shock. "Do you mean there are no haunted castles? No thunderstorms? No abducting and rescuing? Why, Jane, what possessed you to begin such a serious book?"

She responded to my mockery by kicking me gently. I looked at her foot, elegantly shod in one of the soft kid slippers she always wore indoors, aware how much smaller it was than my own.

"It is supposed to be a comedy," she said. "And I must admit that the story is very true to life. There is a family of daughters whose father can leave them no fortune, so they must find rich husbands."

"In that case," I retorted, "male beauty will certainly appear soon. Perhaps in the very next chapter."

"The most beautiful daughter is called … now, let me see." She turned the pages, frowning prettily. "Oh! Her name is Jane! How penetrating this author is!"

She said this with the coyness she had learned from her mama, which never failed to drain my reserve of tolerance. But I collected myself. "Shall we speak of Mr Shelley, or do you not want to hear?"

"I can scarcely contain my impatience!" she said, putting *Pride and Prejudice* aside. "Describe his looks immediately. In every detail, please."

"He has curly hair, quite long, over his collar. And beautiful eyes."

"And are his clothes new, and well kept?"

"Jane! I thought you were a romantic!"

"I assure you I am," she said gently. "But if you are going to fall in love with an earl's son, or whatever he is, do you not think you might make sure he has money, as well as a title?"

I paused before I spoke. "His clothes are shabby, actually. His boots are quite worn out."

"Ah."

"Papa knows he has money, though. I could hear it in his voice when he spoke to him. You know, that way Papa has of speaking to people who admire his work, and whom he considers might be induced to give him financial support."

Jane looked thoughtful. "Mama told Fanny that Papa is in debt for the rent. He has not paid for the shop or the house for six months. Do you suppose he is hoping this Shelley will help him?"

I said nothing. I was surprised enough by this news, without having to consider Shelley's potential involvement.

"But of course ..." said Jane with a sly look, "if he were to become Papa's *son-in-law*..."

"Jane, do not torment me!" I stood up and walked about her room. "I must not invite ridicule by throwing myself at him." I was glad Jane had not witnessed the performance with the ladder. "All he did was remember my name. If you had been there, do you not think he would have done the same for you?"

"No, I do not," she said decisively. "And if we do not receive a call from Lord or Viscount or Whatever-he-is Shelley in the very near future, I will eat this novel, pride and prejudice and all, with potatoes and gravy." She took up the book again. "Now, go away and let me read about the lover of the beautiful Jane. He must surely enter soon!"

Angel

He must surely enter soon.

Every day for three days I sat on the window-seat and watched for Shelley. Naturally I could not mention his name to Papa, and I had no wish to speak it in front of Mama or Fanny. Only Jane shared my secret. The man I marry will…

On the fourth day, he came.

His tie was neat and his jacket had been brushed, and he carried a cane with a silver top. He had a handsomely bound book in the crook of his elbow. When he was shown into the drawing-room, he took little notice of Mama's effusive welcome but handed the book straight to me.

"I understand you are a reader," he said, smiling broadly. "Would you do me the honour of reading this? I am very happy to lend it."

The book was Cowper's *Hymns*. A suitably improving text to give a young girl in the presence of her mother. Mama, admiring the book, drowned my thanks with hers. But as Shelley attended to her I realized he was not attending to her at all. *I care nothing about the book,* he was thinking,

I care only for the girl. How can I get her away from her tiresome mama?

"The day is very fine," he declared when Mama paused. "Might we not take a walk? We are but a few strides from a pleasant churchyard, I notice."

"I do not take walks, sir," said Mama.

I was not inviting you, madam, said Shelley's small, pinched bow.

"But of course my daughters would be happy to accompany you," she continued. "You will take some tea with us first?"

"That would be a pleasure," said Shelley.

"Ring the bell," she instructed me. "And summon Jane and Fanny."

I went to the bell by the fireplace, dismayed. Did she think Shelley wished to escort *all* her daughters?

When Jane and Fanny appeared Shelley bowed, his gaze lingering on Jane's face longer than on Fanny's. Fanny, confronted with an attractive man only a year or two older than herself, flushed. But Jane remained as cool and coquettish as always. I reflected sourly that she must have rehearsed that perfect smile in front of the mirror upstairs, just as I had rehearsed my own less-than-perfect one.

We sat down uncomfortably. While Mama prattled, I examined Shelley.

He was still the angel I had described to Jane, as perfect a specimen of young manhood as I had ever seen. His smooth cheeks and light curls made him look even younger than his years. He held his head nobly, with the air of a man of means and education poised at the beginning of a brilliant career. His tall frame fitted into the armchair without awkwardness.

He nodded as Mama talked, but made little reply.

I looked at his hands. They were bony like the rest of him, and white, with prominent veins. On one of the fingers of his left hand he wore a gold ring. I tried to see the seal, but he put the hand in his pocket suddenly. Perhaps it was not a signet ring, but a family heirloom of some kind. Whatever it was, I was satisfied that Shelley met all my expectations of a suitor. As I passed him a cup of tea, our fingers touched. He caught my eye. I summoned a smile as charming as Jane's, and more sincere.

Then Mama fired an arrow into the conversation.

"May I ask, Mr Shelley," she began, a slice of bread and butter halfway to her mouth, "after the health of *Mrs* Shelley? I hear she is indisposed."

I was standing by the tea tray. During the silence which followed, I sat down shakily on a footstool. I could not look at Jane or Fanny.

Mrs Shelley? She was Shelley's mother, surely. Hope rushed forward eagerly, then retreated again as I recollected that Mama was too much society's slave to neglect anyone's title. As the wife of an earl, Shelley's mother would be referred to as *Lady* Shelley. My thoughts racing, I was forced to conclude that Shelley was, indeed, married. And his wife was *indisposed*. Jane and I knew what was meant by that word, even if our less worldly older sister did not – Mrs Shelley was expecting a baby.

My heart felt ready to burst, but Shelley seemed unembarrassed. He sipped his tea, put down the cup and sat back in his chair as calmly as if my stepmother had remarked upon the weather.

"I thank you for your solicitations," he said. "She is

recovering from the sickness she has suffered recently. Her family is hopeful that she may take a change of air at some coastal town next month."

Mama had swallowed her bite of bread and butter. "And shall your little daughter accompany her?" she asked, tilting her head to one side in a way which might have been attractive twenty years before. "Or is she to be left in the care of her capable papa?"

I stared at her. Then I stared at Shelley. Then I stared at the carpet. Oh God, I thought, what it must be to bear the child of a man like this! And this woman, his wife, had already done so, and was about to do so again!

My head began to ache. If all this were true, why had Shelley taken notice of me in the shop? Why had he come here today? Why, if he was already a husband and father, had he brought me a gift and offered to take me for a walk? The effort of understanding was too great. I felt hot. The pattern on the carpet began to dance, weaving between the legs of the footstool and around the hem of my gown.

Jane and Fanny sat beside each other on a small sofa, Jane alert and interested, Fanny slumped languorously in her seat, her hand resting on Jane's, her face and neck still pink. Now I understood why Mama wanted all of her daughters to accompany Shelley on a walk. The expedition was to be a family outing, with Shelley performing the role of a kindly male visitor taking a trio of spare females for an afternoon stroll.

I drew my shawl more closely around my shoulders. Beneath the thin knitted silk, more fashionable than warm, the flesh on my arms tingled. Though I was sitting on a footstool like a child, at that moment I did not feel like a child.

My heart forced its way into my throat and beat there, forbidding speech. For all my shock at Mama's revelation, I sensed that Shelley's intentions were quite different from hers. I had received his silent communication in the shop, and another just now when he had given me the book. He wanted me. Me, me, *me* and no other.

Rebellion and Respectability

During the next few weeks Shelley called regularly, becoming, in the opinion of my parents, a model of elder-brotherly affection to both Jane and myself. Although it was Papa who hoped to win Shelley as a rich patron, it was Shelley who charmed Papa, spending hours in discussion with him after we ladies had retired from the dining table, and publicly declaring himself a disciple of Papa's ideas about social reform. If Papa suspected the real reason for this blossoming friendship he did not speak of it. He merely basked in Shelley's admiration, trusting that financial support from such a wealthy man would follow.

Jane and I would often accompany Shelley on walks to the churchyard where my mother was buried, the very place he had suggested to Mama on his first visit. He liked to sit with us on a stone bench there, reading poems or telling stories of his exploits.

Having been expelled from university because he refused to believe in God, and thrown off by his rich father, who approved of neither his beliefs nor his lifestyle, he now struggled to provide for himself by publishing poems and relying on the generosity of friends. My father persisted in his belief that Shelley had some money in the form of trusts or legacies, but Shelley did not provide a penny to help with Papa's outstanding rental payments. In view of Shelley's sensational history, his gift of Cowper's *Hymns* was surely a joke.

Most sensationally of all, the story of his wife, Harriet, emerged. It sounded like a fairy tale. He had abducted her from her boarding school three years previously, when she was sixteen and he was nineteen, and had married her despite parental disapproval on both sides. They had had a baby girl, Ianthe, and Harriet was now expecting a second child.

"Sixteen!" exclaimed Jane. "You should be ashamed of yourself!"

Shelley, who was sitting between us on the bench, hung his head. "I *am* ashamed," he confessed. I could tell from his voice, though Jane could not, that he was teasing her. "But I am obliged to bear it as best I can. My susceptibility to sixteen-year-old feminine beauty will not abate, whatever I may do." He raised his eyes to her face, then to mine. "Have you any remedy you might suggest?"

"You are a very bad man!" I scolded. "Have you no pity for my sister's sensibilities? She believes every word you say."

Shelley slid off the bench and knelt on the grass in front of me. "And you do not? Madam, I entreat you, hear me," he said, rolling his eyes theatrically. "I can explain."

Jane and I exchanged amused looks.

"I will hear you," I agreed, "if you will stop these monkey tricks and be serious."

He became serious. He sat cross-legged like a schoolboy, looking from one to the other of us as he spoke. "My wife Harriet and I are estranged. We have not lived together for months. I will not weary you with the details, but I would wager that the unborn child is not mine but her present lover's."

Jane and I both gasped. Then, because this struck us as funny, we laughed at the same time too. And Shelley, who never could remain grave for two minutes, began to laugh, and kissed our hands.

"Why should a man with a miserable marriage," he demanded, "whose wife has wantonly abandoned him for someone else, not enjoy new acquaintance?"

"Acquaintance with sixteen-year-old feminine beauty, that is?" asked Jane archly.

"Of course!" cried Shelley. "I adore you all!"

He might adore us all, but I adored only him. Handsome, brave, rebellious, gifted, and adhering without scruple to the principles of both my parents' writings, he could do no wrong. Freedom for slaves! Freedom for women! Freedom from marriage! Freedom for everyone to love as, when and where they will! And a freedom of his own, his championship of which impressed me more than any other. Freedom for the human race to live without the tyranny of religion!

To my eyes he was beyond doubt a genius.

I did not, indeed I could not, resist his charm. I saw no one but him, dreaming or waking. My eyes did not function unless he was there for them to look at. I fell in love so madly I almost did not recognize it as love. It was madness and nothing else.

Shelley was never unkind to Jane. Indeed, he always treated her like a glittering accessory, a beguiling addition to our party. But as it became more and more obvious that it was *my* "acquaintance" he wanted, I ceased to think about any claim her superior beauty might have on him.

My trusty confidante and I held candlelit meetings in her room, hours after the rest of the household was asleep. Jane sat in the bed, rosy-faced, wearing her coverlet as a cloak, quizzing and scolding me by turns.

"He is the perfect man, Mary, but quite unattainable," she complained. "Why cannot you forget him, and join me in our search for men who are free to marry us? Why have you abandoned your sister's prospects? I call it very selfish!"

"Because I love him."

"But he is married!"

"She has betrayed him."

"And he has no money!"

"Papa thinks he has money."

"Papa is wrong. Do you not recognize a parasite when you see one?"

"Do not call him that!"

"I will call him what I like." She tossed her head, which was covered all over with curl papers. "He is the well-known species of *Parasitus charmingus*, identified by its high degree of personal beauty, large brain and warm heart."

I laughed aloud.

"Shh!" She shook me by the arm. "Do you want to wake them all?"

"Yes," I replied, still laughing. "I want to wake them all and tell them that I am in love!"

Poor Jane had no power to dissuade me from my course.

All of my senses were fine-tuned to squeeze every pleasure from each moment with Shelley. I read and reread his tattered notes, and put them away with sprigs of lavender in a locked box. I spent an embarrassingly long time during one of his visits devising a way to approach him from behind with my sewing scissors, and cut off one of his curls to put in my locket. Then I was too afraid to do it.

Secretly I planned a future with him, Harriet or no Harriet.

He would eventually, I was sure, find a way to marry me. We would make peace with his father and have a large country house and a London apartment, and be at the very centre of society, a world I longed to enter but because of my Radical background had never imagined I would.

In truth, I wanted everything: rebellion and respectability, dreams and reality. An angel and a man.

I dreamt he wrote me a letter.
So perfect a letter, so full of love and joy, that it could only exist in a dream, because real letters are not perfect. They are instruments of torture. They bring promises of meetings, prosperity, new acquaintance, and news of old acquaintance, babies' health, the achievements of sons and the marriages of daughters. They tell of death and despair. But they are insubstantial, untrue, faithless.
Like love itself.

The words in the dream-letter were not ordinary words. I had superhuman powers, which allowed me to lift them physically off the page. Some of them I put in my mouth. They tasted bitter, but I could not spit them out. A pile of them lay on the ground. I plunged my hand into them and scattered them like garden leaves. They settled again in different places, mirror images of themselves, written backwards. Others flew about my face and neck, moth-like, not quite biting me but causing me distress. I exclaimed and pushed them away, but they persisted, and I began to scratch my skin.
All his beautiful words, turning into monster-moths.

Perhaps dreams mean nothing, but this dream was hard to bear. Others may scorn the idea that what we see in life we see in our dreams, horribly twisted out of recognizable shape. But I believe it.

Lover

*H*ow strange. However much we plan, and hope, and map things in our minds, life never reads the same script as we have prepared. It tears up our predictions and laughs at us for presuming to make them.

As spring became summer and the foliage in the church-yard thickened, Shelley and I spent countless hours alone there. He had no profession, no superiors to call him to task, no family commitments to tempt him away. Although he was, by his own and my father's account, an ambitious young man with the future at his feet, he always seemed to have a great deal of spare time to devote to recreation and courtship.

We never went into society. He never took me to the theatre or a ball, or even to dine with his friends. I was far too perfect, he would say, to be shown off to people whose admiration of his "heart's echo", as he called me, would make him jealous.

Privately I suspected this shunning of social events to be due more to his very public estrangement from his wife, and his consciousness that I was the daughter of infamous parents, than jealousy. But I kept my counsel, and went willingly with him to the churchyard whenever the opportunity presented itself.

I was, of course, supposed to be chaperoned. Fanny refused this appointment, so Mama had to rely on Jane. Dear, sly, untrustworthy Jane.

She was our ally. She would pretend to Mama that she was accompanying us, but would walk with us only as far as the end of the street, which Mama could see from her lace-curtained window. Once round the corner Jane would set off to enjoy her own unchaperoned time, having arranged to meet us an hour later in order to walk back with us to the house. A simple deception, but parents, as every sixteen-year-old knows, are simple.

One brilliant June day, when Jane had left us as usual, Shelley and I sought our favourite spot, a clearing in the churchyard shaded by yew trees and hidden from passers-by. Careless of my white gown I sat on the grass among the fragrant trees, my skin warmed by the shadow-dappled sun, my bonnet and parasol discarded beside me.

Shelley dropped his jacket, but remained standing. His face looked troubled. He scanned the view, his hand resting on the back of his neck under his shirt collar. In his other hand was a folded piece of paper.

"You are nervous," I observed.

He did not sit down. "I am not nervous."

"What is the matter, then?"

"I have written a poem."

"Indeed?" This was not unusual. I waited to hear his explanation.

"It is a poem addressed to … to Mary someone."

"Ah."

"Do you wish me to read it to you?"

"Of course, if you will sit down and stop fidgeting."

He sat beside me. On his face was a look of tenderness so clear and youthful, it compelled me to embrace him. I propelled myself into his arms like a spaniel. "I am the Mary someone, am I not?" I demanded.

When he laughed his habit was to open his mouth only slightly, sometimes biting his lower lip, as if he were trying to stifle the laughter. Far from being melancholy, as poets are popularly supposed to be, he was capable of behaving like a spaniel too. "Of course you are. And I hope you know what an honour you receive."

He unfolded the paper. The poem was, indeed, about me. But it did not merely tell of his love. It revealed how deeply he desired me to love *him*. As he read, his voice softened; he was scarcely speaking above a whisper by the time he read,

"Gentle and good and mild thou art,
Nor can I live if thou appear
Aught but thyself, or turn thine heart
Away from me…"

When he finished I was so moved that I could not control my tears, which dripped off the end of my nose in an unladylike stream. I had no handkerchief. Shelley did not laugh, but grinned with such profound affection that I forgot how ridiculous I must look and accepted his offer of the end of his tie to wipe my face with. He never had a handkerchief either.

"Oh, Shelley!" I said, when I could speak. "Are these beautiful verses to be published?"

He was sitting cross-legged as usual, looking for all the world like the poor boy Aladdin from the *Thousand and One Nights*. Unkempt, expectant, on the verge of discovering treasure in an unexpected place. He folded the poem and put it in the pocket of his jacket which lay beside him on the grass. Then he caught me round the waist very tightly, so that I could not push him away. He pressed my head to his chest. Beneath my ear, through the thin linen of his shirt, I felt his heart's regular beat, and the rise and fall of his chest as he breathed.

"No, they will not be published. As long as I have a wife living, anyway," he added, and kissed me.

I received the kiss, feeling hot. I wished he would not hold me quite so tightly. My corset was digging into my flesh and I could not get my breath. But Shelley did not appear to notice my discomfort. He brought his face close to mine.

"The fact that I am much more in love with you than I could ever be with Harriet, or any other woman, will not hinder the progress of scandal. So, my dearest Mary, these lines are ours, and ours alone. They mark today as a special day, which I would not want the public to have knowledge of."

I swallowed. I still could not breathe freely. But I could not move, and had abandoned all thought of doing so. "A special day?" I echoed.

"Yes…"

He kissed me again. This kiss was more purposeful than the previous one. My head felt heavy, and full of some substance which obscured my wits. I could not think. I could not find my conscience. I saw his smile widen. How happy and beautiful he was! Desire rushed over my body, as recklessly as a stream splashes over rocks.

"Today is my birthday," he said, laughing. "I am twenty-two today."

He took my face in his hands. My unbalanced brain did not work properly. I found myself trying to kiss his fingers, though my lips could not possibly reach them.

"Can you imagine what is the very best, the most beautiful birthday present you could give me?" he asked.

I was too close to him to see what he was doing, and too intoxicated to protest. My dress disappeared from my shoulders. I was sure I had not loosened it, nor taken the pins from my hair.

"I will remember this day for ever, dearest girl," he told me, and pushed me gently backwards on the grass.

I had lost my powers of reasoning. I was beyond resistance. Shelley and I were the only living things in a world full of unfeeling creatures. The grass and trees, the churchyard, even the sky, disappeared. I was not aware of pain, or even of the ecstasy Jane had unreliably informed me I would feel at this moment. I was aware only that I was with the man I loved in a place from which there was no escape.

And all the time Shelley and I were celebrating his birthday, Jane sat, waiting in the church porch without her bonnet on, her small, finely-shod feet crossed and her ringlets resting innocently against her cheek.

Master

*O*ur idyll was short-lived. No more than a month later I was summoned to the drawing-room to hear that someone – nameless, of course – had seen me walking in the churchyard with Mr Shelley, unchaperoned.

I could not tell which face was redder: my stepmother's quivered with anger, but the origins of my father's heightened colour lay in embarrassment. I was sorry for him, but I was stubborn too.

"I do not deny that I sent Jane away," I declared. I had no wish to fuel my stepmother's fury by implicating her daughter. "She is not to blame. And I am not afraid to admit my feelings for Shelley. As for his feelings for me…"

"They do not exist, I tell you!" broke in Mama. She was in distress, her hands clutching at her gown. "He asked to call, he brought you a book, he wandered in the square and the churchyard with you and Jane a few times. He took tea with me here and dined with us. That is not *love*, you simpleton." She sat down heavily on the sofa. "You do it, William," she instructed my father. "I can speak to her no longer."

My father contemplated me for a few moments. "My dear child…"

"Ach!" said my stepmother in disgust, and turned her face to the peacock-covered cushions.

"My dear child," my father began again. "I fear you do not understand the seriousness of this situation."

"What situation, Papa? That I have fallen in love with a young man who has fallen in love with me?"

"Yes, that situation. And no, not that one."

"Get on with it!" demanded Mama.

"As you know, the young man in question, Mr Shelley, cannot make you his wife," said my father. "He is already married, although it is true that he and his wife are estranged."

"It is true," put in Mama, "that he abandoned her to misery and humiliation!"

I could not allow this. "It is *not* true!" I protested. "She has turned to another man, and is carrying his child."

My father looked at me with pity. "Mary, there is no doubt over the paternity of Mrs Shelley's second baby. She was already with child when her husband left her."

"I do not believe you."

I knew my father's intolerance of scenes, so was resolved upon keeping my temper and countenance. My tone was measured, my voice calm. I could not tell them that my "friendship" with Shelley had already become much more than that, and that I had reason to believe there would shortly be another child to consider, of whose paternity there was also no doubt whatsoever. The complexities of Shelley's private life were more sensational than they, or anyone, knew.

"I know more of what has happened between him and his wife than you do," I continued. "You are repeating rumours in a way that grieves me, and will grieve Shelley when I tell him."

"Grieve Shelley?" said Mama scornfully. "And so it should!" She snapped her fan shut in a way that could have only been designed to irritate and pointed it at me. "You must never see him again. I forbid it." She glanced at my father. "Your papa forbids it. You will stay at home and help in the shop, and Mr Shelley will be prevented from visiting. This situation is intolerable. We shall be the laughing-stock of London."

"Mama is concerned for your reputation," said my father.

"No she is not!" The bitter words came out before I could stop them. "She is concerned for her *own* reputation, just as you are concerned for *yours*!"

The colour faded from Papa's face. "My dear," he said, taken aback, "I assure you that is not the case."

"I do not want your assurances!" My resolve to avoid a scene was faltering. "I want to know why you consider it so scandalous that Shelley should fall in love with me! I am not a fool, Papa. I know that when you married my mama she was already carrying me, and that she was never married to Fanny's father at all. How can you disapprove so violently of *my* conduct?"

He paused before he spoke. When he did, his voice was icy. "You do not understand, child."

"I do, Papa! I understand that you do not want your principles of freedom to extend to me and Shelley. To me because I am your daughter, and to Shelley because you persist in considering him as a benefactor, and you do not want your financial association with him tarnished in any way!"

"Silence!"

He was rarely angry, and I was frightened at the severity of his countenance.

"Papa," I ventured, "I do not wish to make an enemy of you. But I will not give Shelley up. I am resolved."

"Resolved upon ruin!" interjected Mama. "William, the girl has taken leave of her senses."

"Shelley is not what you think, Mama!" I protested. "He will care for me, and as soon as he is free of his wife he will marry me!"

They both looked at me as if I had, indeed, taken leave of my senses.

"Is that truly what you believe?" my father asked. He was staring at me without blinking. "Does it not occur to you that you are the *second* young lady, barely out of childhood, whom this man has pursued? What induces you to think that *you* will fare any better than poor Harriet?"

I was ready with my answer. "Because he loves me and not her!"

"And do you not think he loved her when they eloped?"

Frustration is ugly in a girl of sixteen. I clenched my fists, and my face grew heated. "But he had not met *me* then!" I cried. "If he had, he would never have considered Harriet. Why do you not understand that I love and trust him?"

I looked imploringly at Papa. "Did you never love my mama enough to trust her? Do you not want me to be happy?"

Throughout this outburst my father had watched me, his

expression saddening. When I was silent, and had begun to cry, he took my hand.

"Mary, my dear, I *do* want you to be happy. But Shelley is not the man to give you the happiness I would wish for. He is not honourable – no, do not protest. We none of us know everything about him. He tells us only what he wants to. He is wealthy but uses his money in a profligate manner. Do you honestly wish to attach yourself to this man?"

I did not hesitate. "Yes, sir, I do."

As I sat there in the drawing-room with my small hand enveloped by my father's large one, the rebellion which had long been stirring inside me surfaced. There was no escaping the truth that Shelley *had* eloped with a willing sixteen-year-old. But now he had another willing sixteen-year-old to elope with. Indeed, he had two. We could not leave Jane, our little accomplice, to face my parents' wrath alone.

My father rose abruptly, and was about to quit the room when Jane opened the door without knocking. She had been crying. In her hand was a letter. She seized my hand and thrust the letter into it.

"He is waiting in the shop! Quick, read this and go to him. Quick, quick!"

"Why are you crying?" I asked her, mystified.

Mama was hurrying towards me. "Give me that letter!" she demanded. "I suppose he thinks himself very clever, to have got in by the shop door!"

Jane stood between me and her mother. "I cannot imagine it needed much ingenuity to enter a shop during trading hours, Mama," she said.

"Insolence!" She tried to get past, but Jane barred her way. I unfolded the letter.

Dearest,

Have no fear of what your parents say they will do. We shall still be together, I promise you. Jane shall bring your letters to me, and mine to you. She is a dear girl. Please forgive me for causing you all this distress. I did not know I would fall in love with you so hopelessly, and by the time I had, I was far beyond being able to let you go. Please, please write.

Your true love, Shelley

At the same moment that Mama at last succeeded in twisting the letter out of my grasp, we heard footsteps climbing the uncarpeted stairs from the shop. Jane yelped in dismay, but I was filled suddenly with the strength which passion bestows. I threw open the drawing-room door, neither caring what my parents saw nor what they thought of it.

Shelley was standing in the hall with one hand holding his hat and the other on the back of his neck. The sight of this familiar gesture filled my heart, and I ran into his embrace as if I belonged there. I *did* belong there. I held him tightly, speaking close to his ear. "What will you do? Will you take me far away, to France, or farther? Do you know that Jane speaks perfect French? Please, please let us go away from here!"

He released me. Mama shouted for him to quit the house. But he strode into the drawing-room and faced her and my father without fear.

"Madam, be quiet, if you please," he instructed. "I wish to bid farewell to my future wife in peace. Yes, by God, I *will* marry Mary!"

Mama was shocked into silence. Jane, who was still half-crying, put her hand over her mouth.

"And as for you, sir," said Shelley sternly to my father, "if you abided by your principles you would not object to anything that has passed between your daughter and me. A man should not be bound by the shackles of marriage if he finds a superior love."

My father did not reply.

"Make way," ordered Shelley. "I will take my leave now."

He bowed to them, and, turning to me, kissed my hand. His eyes said, "I will never be allowed into this house again, even through the shop!", as he spoke aloud, "I hope to see you all on a happier day. Until then, goodbye."

Mistress

*A*t first it was a game. Intoxicated with freedom, our spirits remained high all the way to Dover in the carriage, and all the way to Calais on the boat.

I will never forget the sight of Jane on the windy deck, her bonnet-strings flapping about her chin, clutching her wayward skirts, screaming with laughter. And Shelley, his hair wild, his eyes wilder, roaring poetry, the words whipped this way and that by the gale. I held his arm so tightly I could feel his bones through his flesh, shirt, jacket and greatcoat. I was drowning in love.

At the inn in Calais, Shelley and I were too excited to feel tired.

"Tonight is our wedding night!" he said, laughing and kissing me. "Although, of course, we had no wedding…"

"And, of course, you are about to find that your bride is no virgin…"

"And yet her virginity is mine," he replied softly.

My heart began to thump. If only Jane could hear Shelley when he was at his most romantic!

"The whole world will know I am no virgin now we have eloped," I reminded him.

He ceased his kisses. "Oh, Mary! Does it trouble you that you are a ruined woman?"

"Not at all. A ruined reputation is without doubt the only kind to have."

"You will go to hell, dearest."

"You don't believe in hell, *dearest*, so how can I go there?"

Very late, I awoke from a brief sleep to find that Shelley had opened our bedroom shutters to the moonlight. He looked pensive but released from care. Reaching for his travel-stained shirt, he pulled it on over his head like a child.

"Why have you no nightshirt?" I asked.

"Because I have lived so long with nobody to see to such things. I was cast adrift. But now you are my anchor, and I am cold. Warm me up."

It was late July. The cheap room, high up in the eaves, was airless. But I put my arms around him and we lay and talked, and he took me and ruined my reputation further, and we talked more.

I did not tell him about our baby. I wanted to keep the news inside me, as deeply embedded as the child itself, until the moment came to reveal it. My happiness was real, but even on that momentous night I was aware of the ease with which happiness, like other fragile objects, can be destroyed. What had happened, I wondered, to the happiness of Harriet Shelley, in the arms of whose husband I now lay?

As the sky lightened over the roofs of Calais, Shelley slept. I lay curled up, my arms around him under the dirty shirt. He turned onto his back, snuffling like a dog. His head lolled off the bolster. He did not look handsome, but the sight of him stabbed me with desire.

Angel, lover, master. All these adored things, until a few weeks ago utterly unknown, lay beside me in this foreign bed. The fancy came to me that Shelley, too, was as safe and adored as a baby inside its mother. My love was stronger than my parents' outrage, or Harriet's prior claim, or Shelley's father's dismissal of him. Only death, I was convinced, would part us from one another. I kissed his unshaven cheek.

But it was not my kiss that awoke him. The sound of raised voices made us sit up. Groaning, Shelley put his head in his hands.

Mama had pursued us. She was arguing with the landlady in the fluent French she had learned in her youth and taught to Jane. Her voice was accompanied by the noise of the ebony handle of her best parasol repeatedly striking the door of Jane's chamber, which lay opposite ours.

She began to shriek in English, "Jane! Jane! I command you to see me!" Another parasol strike. "If you do not open the door, I will have this woman instruct her servant to break it down!" Two more strikes, then what sounded like a kick with a stout boot. "Open the door this minute!"

The cacophony was enough to wake everyone in Calais. Shelley slid out of bed and looked through the keyhole. He put his finger to his lips, stifling giggles. His bare feet noiseless on the wooden floor, he mimed Mama's shuffling gait. He tied imaginary bonnet strings and waved an invisible parasol. I stuffed the corner of the sheet into my mouth.

Then all was quiet. I heard a door slam and the landlady's footsteps descend the stairs. "Jane has let her in," I whispered. "What shall we do?"

Shelley was putting on his clothes. "*We* shall do nothing," he told me with authority. "*I* can deal with this."

"But she is *my* stepmama, so —"

"You and Jane are my responsibility." He was bending towards the mirror, hastily brushing his hair, and the shoulders of his coat, with my hairbrush. He inspected his reflection. "But if your stepmother thinks I intend to take *her* along with my two dear girls…" He looked at me in horror. "Get dressed and meet us downstairs. She will be on the next sailing home." He struck the hairbrush defiantly upon his other palm. "And without Jane, I give you my word."

He was just in time. Mama and Jane emerged from the room opposite as he opened our door. Both saw me in the instant before he closed it again. Both conveyed messages — contempt on Mama's part, anguish on Jane's. I did what Shelley had instructed; stepping into my travelling gown, I fairly flew down the stairs and tumbled into the public room of the inn.

"Mama…" I began, but Shelley gestured to me to be silent.

He was standing at the empty fireplace, his hands in his pockets, his eyes alight. Mama's bulky form filled an armchair. Jane, her luggage at her feet, wept softly into a handkerchief.

Poor Jane, I thought. She loves to imagine fictional dramatic scenes but is powerless to deal with a real one.

"I insist upon it, Mr Shelley," Mama was saying. "I must save my own daughter from the clutches of infamy while I can." She nodded in my direction. "My stepdaughter's fate is out of my hands, but Jane has nothing to do with you."

Shelley did not reply. Mama's eyes held his face in a cold, quivering stare. "You are yourself the parent of a daughter, Mr Shelley. Would you not, in similar circumstances, do the same for her?"

I thought Shelley would buckle under this sly thrust at his own parental responsibility. But my anxiety was unfounded.

"You are correct, madam, in one particular," he said. "I *am* the parent of a beloved daughter, to be sure. But my wish for Ianthe is joy greater even than that which your stepdaughter has given me. If, in willingly fleeing her family for new friends, she found the happiness lacking at home, I would give her my blessing!"

Mama's outrage filled the room. She stood up.

"How dare you, sir? How dare you – *you*, of all people – accuse me of making my daughter unhappy? All you know is profligacy, adultery, seduction! And may God have mercy on you when your time comes!"

Trembling, stumbling over the hem of her gown, she hauled Jane to her feet. "Come, Jane, let us leave this place with dignity!"

There was no sound except Jane's strenuous sobbing. She went with her mother to the street door. The carriage Mama had hired was waiting outside.

My feelings were stirred. Here, in this crudely furnished inn room, I saw for the first time what it might be like to be the protector of my own child. Would Shelley, with his fierce love for his little daughter, ever fight to preserve her honour as my father had fought to preserve mine, and as Mama now fought to preserve Jane's? I looked at him, my eyes stinging. He neither moved nor spoke. I could not read his feelings.

Then Mama, stepping into the carriage first, released Jane's arm and Shelley saw his opportunity. He seized my sister, sweeping her feet from under her.

Surprise made her scream, but within an instant she put one arm tightly around his neck. "Oh, Shelley!" she cried. "How brave you are!"

"Quick, Mary, coins!" panted Shelley.

I understood, and pressed some sous into Jane's outstretched hand. As Shelley bore her away, she threw the coins at the carriage man's feet, giving him rapid instructions in French.

He nodded, kicked the carriage steps up and closed the door.

"Au revoir, Maman!" called Jane. *"Bon voyage!"*

The driver whipped up the horses. Mama's face, consumed by fury, appeared briefly at the window. Then she was gone.

Shelley deposited Jane on the cobblestones. "Can you not picture her," he grinned, "pounding the roof of the carriage with her parasol, shouting to the driver to stop?"

"He will not stop," Jane assured him, her tears drying on her cheeks and her eyes ablaze with admiration for Shelley. "I told him she has the cholera, and must be put on the first sailing, whatever her protests, to rid France of the infection she may spread."

I had surveyed this scene from the door of the inn. Now I descended the steps and took Shelley's arm. "You should invest in a parasol yourself, Shelley," I suggested. "*That* would surely give the gossips something to talk about!"

The Two-headed Goddess

From Calais we went to Paris. Then we travelled farther and farther south.

Shelley had left a forwarding address, and at the hotel in Grenoble, near the Swiss border, we picked up letters. The three of us took them up to the bedchamber Shelley and I shared.

"This is from Fanny," I said as I broke the seal on the only letter addressed to me.

Shelley heard my dismay and looked up from his own letters. But before I could speak, nausea rose. I felt hot. My ears buzzed. Unable to support myself, I leant against the back of his chair. I still had not told anyone about the child, but the child was telling me constantly of its presence. Pretending the French food did not agree with me was making Jane very suspicious.

They both looked at me. "What is it, my love?" asked Shelley. "Come, sit down."

He pulled me onto his lap. Fanny's letter fell unread from my fingers.

"Shelley, are you blind?" Jane demanded. "Can you not see that your 'love' is in the same condition as your wife?"

He looked at me with his abandoned-child look. "Are you, Mary?"

I nodded, ashamed, ready to cry.

"Why have you not disclosed this sooner?" he asked. "My dear, I have not been caring for you and the child properly! You must not walk so much! You must have a horse, or a carriage!"

"We have not the money for a carriage," observed Jane.

Ignoring her, he caressed my face and hair. I accepted the caresses gratefully, wetting his collar with my tears. Then I blew my nose on Jane's handkerchief, and felt better.

Shelley was smiling broadly. "Our own child!" He squeezed me. "How delightful it will be to have our own child! Are you not happy?"

"Of course I am happy. And so relieved!"

While I had been crying, Jane, who had never had any scruples about invading my privacy, had picked up Fanny's letter. She took it closer to the window. *"I hope this letter does not find you as it leaves me,"* she read. *"I am greatly distressed by a rumour which is circulating in London, and of which I feel I must warn you."*

"Only *one* rumour!" said Shelley good-naturedly.

"Shelley's wife, Harriet, has been gossiping," read Jane. *"She is telling everyone that Papa allowed you and Jane to go off with Shelley for the price of fifteen hundred pounds. In other words, that he sold you."*

There was an astounded silence. My instinct was to laugh, but Shelley's expression became serious. He slapped the table with the palm of his hand. "Harriet!" he exclaimed.

"Treacherous, infantile, gossiping wretch!"

As he stood up, I slid off his lap onto his vacant chair. He snatched the letter angrily from Jane. "Fifteen hundred pounds!" he cried. "*Fifteen hundred pounds!* Can you bear to listen to this poison, Mary? I will never forgive her!"

"Harriet seeks not forgiveness," observed Jane calmly, "but revenge. And if anyone believes that our father could do such a thing then they are ignorant scandalmongers worthy only of contempt."

Shelley looked at her with interest. The flickering candle threw shadows on his face, and in his expression I read indignation but also mischief.

"I am shocked, indeed," he said gravely, turning to the letter once more. "But what truly aggrieves me is the amateur quality of Harriet's gossiping. Does she not care to find out the true sum, before she spreads the rumour abroad?"

Jane was staring at him. "What do you mean?"

"I mean that Harriet knows nothing of her own husband's talent for business," he said. "I would be a scoundrel indeed if I took two daughters off an honest man for anything less than *ten thousand* pounds!"

Jane gasped. Her small white hand flew to her small pink mouth. Above it her eyes bulged, full of delight and dread.

Poor Jane. She was the perfect butt of everyone's teasing, always taking the bait and never understanding the joke. I had lived with this characteristic too long to find it entertaining, but for Shelley it was a novelty.

Suppressing an interruption from me, he leant towards her, highly amused. "Think, Jane!" he commanded. "Your papa, having extracted ten thousand pounds from his unhappy benefactor, may now pay his rent arrears fifty times over, and take new premises in a smarter district into the bargain!"

"Shelley, stop!" I scolded.

But he could not stop. Once a joke had suggested itself, he was unable to resist stretching it to its limits. He capered around the room like a drunkard, howling. My remonstrations merely added to the noise.

"How much for an arm or a leg?" he bellowed. "How much for a heart? Or a nostril? Or the nail of a great toe, indeed!"

In the midst of this madness sat Jane, pouting like a child. She was still not certain that Shelley was joking. I could guess what her gullible mind was imagining: Shelley and our father arguing about whether the daughter who shared Shelley's bed was worth a larger proportion of the ten thousand pounds than the one who did not, then Papa slapping Shelley on the back, and shaking his hand, and signing a document.

Anxiety, mingled with suspicion, showed so plainly in her face that I took pity on her. "Jane, you goose!" I chided. "Have no fear that Shelley is serious. Do you not know by now what a jester he is?"

But suspicion, once aroused, is difficult to disperse. Warily she watched Shelley's laughter ebb and disappear, and his face compose itself again.

"Why do you use me thus, you wicked man?" she asked him sharply, like a governess interrogating her charge. Jane would make a good governess, I had often thought.

Shelley bowed, then raised his eyes to her face without lifting his head. He looked like a wayward servant abasing himself before his mistress. "I do it because I *can*," he admitted. "Because Mary is too astute to be taken in."

"And I am *not* astute, I suppose?" demanded Jane.

"You are innocent, my dear." As he said this he bowed lower, and kissed her hand. Into his eyes came a look I knew, loved, and dreaded. "And when we find innocence in this corrupt world, must we not cherish it?"

Jane rose and smoothed her skirt. There was agitation in her eyes. "We have an early start in the morning," she said. "I am going to bed now, and I suggest you do the same."

When she had left the room Shelley knelt beside my chair and put his head in my lap. "*Am* I a wicked man, Mary?"

"Of course you are," I told him solemnly. "Why else do you think I love you?"

He raised his head. "Thank Providence you do," he said softly. "Otherwise, I would be lost."

I could not do otherwise than believe him. But I was capable of greater penetration even than he knew; I had seen that he needed something I was unable to provide. He loved me, but he resisted what he had tactfully called my "astute" nature. Equally tactfully he had referred to Jane's slower intelligence as "innocence", a quality I transparently lacked, but which he nevertheless found temptingly attractive.

His poems were full of immortal visions of feminine beauty. But could it be that Jane and I furnished him with a two-headed goddess more divine than any in his imagination? In us, had he found one perfect mistress?

His curly hair felt warm beneath my palm. A dart of affection entered my heart, and I bent and kissed him. As I caressed him, and watched his eyes soften like a dreamer's, I told myself that jealousy is a madness greater even than the madness of love. And there is no escape from its torture.

Shelley, Jane and I were chained to one another, as

securely as prisoners. Tomorrow we would continue our journey into Switzerland. The humdrum life Jane and I had known in England lay behind us. What lay before us, we could not know. Our fate was in the lap not of the gods, but of the two-headed goddess.

Concubine

Switzerland is a country of such dazzling beauty that every day unfolds a new joy. To live amid such glory is privilege enough, but to see it for the first time when already intoxicated with love, and in the company of the beloved, is heaven.

One evening, Shelley was sitting with his hand under the collar of his shirt, casting his eyes over the splendour of the Alpine view. Deep-blue shadows lengthened beneath the mountains. Green fields, bedecked with flowers, sloped to a lake which displayed a perfect upside-down picture of the peaks and the purpling sky. Beside him on the grass sat my sister and I in equal contentment.

To a passing stranger our party must have seemed mysterious in its composition. Two ladies, similarly dressed in muslin and light shawls, drinking wine with a man too young to be their father, too well-dressed to be their manservant, too affectionate to be their brother. The pretty face of one of these ladies was shaded by a bonnet, the brim of which was adorned with local flowers, but the other displayed to the world her bright red-gold hair, pinned up in windswept strands that had earlier been curls.

"Who is for a ghost story?" asked Shelley, pouring the last dregs of wine. "I can think of no better way to pass the hours before bedtime."

"Oh, yes!" enthused Jane. "I have no inclination to return early to that sluttish landlady's filthy rooms."

"No more have I," I agreed. "Last night Shelley found a bedbug the size of a halfpenny crawling up his arm."

"Shelley, dear," Jane urged, turning to him, "tell a really frightening ghost story! Make my flesh creep!"

Jane and I had always delighted in feeling our flesh creep. Papa's mild disapproval had never discouraged us from reading every horror novel we could obtain – fashionable and unfashionable, of literary merit or otherwise. In Jane's room, by the light of the dying embers of her fire, our education had been enriched by haunted castles, bloodthirsty murders, torture and depravity of a considerably more violent nature than Papa ever knew. These were subjects very appealing to our young minds, and much more entertaining than the needlework we always managed to "forget" to do.

Shelley was a showman, especially after wine. He jumped up and spread his arms wide.

"Indeed, can you imagine a more appropriate setting for a ghost story?" he asked. "Behold, the lake! The mountains! The cobblestones! The gathering dusk! The picturesque pony and cart winding its way up the incline…"

"But to the *story*, Shelley…" encouraged Jane.

He smiled conspiratorially, taking a leather-bound volume from his pocket. Shelley was never, ever without a book about his person. Usually poetry, but on this occasion a collection of ghost stories.

"Steel your nerves, ladies," he warned us.

As the darkness gathered above the lake, the mountains disappeared and the village street emptied. Flickering candles began to appear at windows. No pony hooves or nailed boots broke the silence. Shelley's voice was the only one we heard.

But while he read well, I found myself less interested in the story than in Jane's conduct. I watched her edge gradually nearer Shelley until her leg pressed his. Both his hands were occupied in holding the book and turning the pages, but she found some exposed flesh between his wrist and his shirt cuff, which he had pushed a few inches up his arm. Jane's excited fingers encircled his forearm, and she leant towards him, exaggerating her décolletage by squeezing her upper arms close to her sides.

Breathing in little gasps, she hung not only on his arm, but also his words. As the tale progressed to its gory climax, she began to protest prettily, with fluttering hands and brimming eyes.

"Stop! Stop!" she begged. "I am too weak for this. Forgive me!"

Shelley went to shut the book, but Jane's hand darted out to prevent him. "Oh, but I wish to hear the end of the story!"

She was playing on Shelley's conviction that she was a fool. She was begging him to forgive her susceptibility to nervous hysteria while encouraging him to continue with the very thing that caused it. It was a perfect example of the helpless idiocy which he found so attractive.

But she was *not* a fool. I myself had schooled her for years in impressing her beauty and charm upon men. How could I be surprised that Shelley had become the focus of everything she had learned? Or that she had assumed the role of concubine, hoping he would soon lose interest in the loyal, less alluring "wife" who was carrying his child?

My elopement with Shelley lives in my memory as a summer studded with brilliant sights and experiences, and hour upon hour of happiness. But equally vivid is the mistrust which tugged pitilessly at my heart. Dear God, how I regretted the generosity of spirit I had shown in pressing my sister to accompany us!

I went to bed that night consumed with indignation. I could not frame the words to confront Shelley with my feelings. But a few hours later I discovered that Jane had further ammunition in her campaign to capture him.

It was after midnight when we were woken by the door of our chamber being flung open. Jane tumbled into the room, gibbering like a madwoman.

"The furniture in my bedroom is moving!" she announced. "Every time I lie down it takes one more pace towards me, as if it would crush me!"

I was unimpressed by this display of feigned insanity. "You have taken too much wine," I declared. "Go back to bed."

But she would not be turned away. "Mary!" she begged, plucking at our blankets. "Have you no pity? I cannot sleep in that room. I shall have to sleep in here!"

And before either of us could stop her, she threw back the covers on Shelley's side and joined us in the bed.

But Shelley was equally unimpressed. Solemnly he climbed over me and got out of my side of the bed.

"Mary, I am going to sleep in Jane's room," he informed me.

"You are not afraid of living furniture, then?" I asked dryly.

"I am anxious only for sleep." He padded across the room. "And for pity's sake, keep your sister in here."

"Shelley!" shrieked Jane as the door closed behind him. "Shelley, do not leave me!"

"Quiet!" I commanded. "I have endured enough of your histrionics."

By this time my vision had become accustomed to the darkness and I could see her eyes glittering in the pale glow of moonlight. She could see me too. I could imagine the picture I presented: my hair hung in strands around my face, and I was wearing an old chemise as a nightdress. But every fibre of my body was roused to the fight.

"Your pursuit of a man who is in love with someone else is pitiful!" I told her.

"Witch!" she hissed. "How can you think he loves *you*?"

"I *know* he loves me! The greater question is, how can you think he wants *you*?"

"Because he said so!" she blurted.

I stared at her in horror. The only thing that had preserved my sanity during these last weeks had been the sight of Shelley responding to her onslaughts with derision or bewilderment, if he responded at all. But when I was not looking, had he truly confessed his desire for her?

"There!" she declared triumphantly. "Put that in your witch's cauldron and stir it!"

"Tell me his words!" I demanded. "If this is true, tell me exactly what he said, and I will challenge him!"

"Oh, Mary!" She fell back onto the pillow, her hands pressed to her temples. "Is it not you who has always said, 'A man needs no words to describe desire'? It is so obvious he prefers me, a child could see it!"

My alarm subsided. She was lying, then. If he really *had* spoken, she would be carrying the words engraved on her memory.

"Jane, your immorality knows no bounds," I told her. I took her tightly by the shoulders. "Are you listening to me?"

She yelped with affected pain. "Leave me alone!"

"Gladly, but not until I have said this." I gripped her tighter; I think I probably *was* hurting her. "I wish you had never come with us. I wish Shelley had never bothered to rescue you from Mama in Calais, and that she had taken you home and locked you in your room, like the child you are."

She was crying now, as noisily as any child.

"Your lies about Shelley are ridiculous. How Shelley will laugh when I tell him!"

Her wails stopped. It was her turn to look horrified.

"Yes, I will tell him!" I assured her.

"Oh, Mary, you are cruel!"

I let go of her shoulders. I felt not a shred of sympathy for her tears.

"Now, stop this performance and go to sleep," I said firmly. "Shelley will not be back tonight."

He, at least, got some sleep. I got none. Jane inflicted her disappointment on me all night, alternately sobbing and snoring and almost suffocating me every time she rolled over.

The Spark of Being

*L*ack of funds soon meant we had to forgo our hired carriage and travel by cheaper means. I was too tired to walk far. Shelley's boots had holes in them. Jane, out of spirits and no longer flirting with Shelley, complained endlessly. Eventually we realized that we could not drift about Europe for ever, pursued by scandal and beset by poverty. We would have to go home.

Shelley proposed to take us back to England by riverboat, sailing up the Rhine to Holland, and from there across the Channel. But for me, with nausea a daily burden, even the prospect of travelling by river – I could not contemplate the sea – was unattractive.

"I will not go," I declared.

He and I were dining at yet another inn, on food as ill-cooked as we had come to expect. Jane had not appeared at the table. I was feeling low and could not eat.

"But Mary, my dear," protested Shelley. "Do you not want to feel the fresh air on your face, and see beautiful scenery?"

"No," I told him.

"Then consider this," he persisted, taking my hand: "we shall be sailing towards the sea. I am done with Switzerland, notwithstanding the wondrous Alps, because the sea is so far away, and sailing is such a pleasure!"

I regarded him doubtfully.

"The wildness of the sea is in an Englishman's blood," he continued, patting my hand enthusiastically. "The River Rhine, majestic though it may be, provides no competition for the thunderous music of the waves."

I pondered. "We three – you, Jane and I – are like the sea, do you not think? We have no beginning and no end. We come from nowhere and are going nowhere. We are vagabonds. We are outcasts."

Shelley always grew impatient when I spoke of my feelings of exile. He dropped my hand. "We are *not*. When we arrive in England, our families –"

"Our families have already disowned us."

"Do not say that! Your father will welcome his child's safe return, as any decent man would." He saw my sadness, and softened his voice. "I promise you, my love, that the outdoor life will agree with you. Nature always compensates for the miseries of mankind."

The next day we boarded the passenger vessel that was to take us to Holland. The weather was indeed kind, and soon the loveliness of the Rhineland and the revival of spirits offered by mild air and daily exercise restored me. I began once more to drown in love.

Shelley appeared to be drowning too; he did not let his enthusiasm for river traffic and ruined castles distract his attention from me. We spent many hours strolling up and down the deck, his arm around my waist, talking of plans for the birth of our child and our future life together.

And what of Jane? She remained the same sister I had grown up with: pert yet artless, knowing yet naïve, trustworthy yet treacherous. Forced into the role of unpaid companion to a pregnant sister and a man who would not take his attraction further than flirtation, she had to retreat. Much of the time she stayed below in her cabin, shunning the sunlight, nursing schemes which only God was privy to. I was not sorry.

The Rhine cuts a deep chasm through wooded hills. As our vessel meandered its way northwards, we glimpsed great houses between the trees. Tiny villages and larger towns lined the cliff-tops, spilling like foam to the water's edge. Every few miles we would pass below a castle on a rocky promontory, sometimes inhabited, but more often the ruined relic of medieval wars.

One evening, near sunset, the boat moored beneath a spectacular castle. Most of the passengers came out on deck to look at it, several sitting down to sketch it. Jane stayed below, saying she had some letters to write.

Warmed by the dying sunlight, I fell asleep in a chair on deck. When I awoke Shelley was admiring the sketch an elderly German man was making. Shelley spoke little German, but the man seemed to have fluent English.

"This castle is very interesting, my dear sir," he told Shelley.

The castle looked very romantic, with the late sun gilding its towers. Surrounded by heavily wooded countryside, it looked a perfect medieval fortress. But, like most of the others, it was a ruin.

"The man who lived there was an alchemist," the elderly gentleman was saying.

I sat up. Who could not be fascinated by the idea of alchemy, the power to turn base metal into gold? The search for its secret had occupied men for centuries, and continued to do so. "What happened to him, sir?" I asked.

"Oh, you are awake!" exclaimed Shelley affectionately. "This is Herr Keffner, my dear."

The man bowed and addressed me politely, taking me for Shelley's wife.

"Please," I repeated, "tell us about the alchemist."

Herr Keffner looked into my face with watery blue eyes. He was perhaps seventy years old, but as trim and well worn as his walking-stick. "More than an alchemist," he said. "A scientist, and a ... what is the English word? A lunatic?"

"That word will do," agreed Shelley, with a glance at me. "For poets as much as for scientists!"

"He lived more than a hundred years ago. In those days people truly believed in alchemy, but this man also had another, more deranged idea. He believed that if you took the body parts of dead people, and joined them together, you could bring the resulting creation to life."

We were silent. At my shoulder I sensed Shelley's tightening attention. "Jane would love to hear this," I whispered to him. "The bloodier the better."

I again addressed Herr Keffner. "Sir, if you please, did this gentleman ever succeed in carrying out his gory experiment?"

"Yes, indeed. He robbed graves for the materials, and if he could not find human remains he used the bones of animals."

I asked the questions I could not contain. "How did he propose to bring them to life? And how did he justify his actions, morally? Can it be right to bestow the spark of being on matter which God has deemed should die?"

Herr Keffner gave Shelley an amused glance. "I see your wife is a philosopher," he said. "It is unusual to hear a lady speak of such things."

"That may be true in Germany," replied Shelley, "but in England we have many women of fine intelligence who question the judgement of men. I am proud to hear my wife speak so."

The German bowed his head politely. "The alchemist sought to inject the flesh with a potion, made with blood and other substances," he explained. "I need not tell you that he did not succeed, and died raving."

"Poor man," I observed. "To have such a dream, and be disappointed."

"Indeed," agreed Herr Keffner.

He fell silent, and continued with his drawing. Shelley and I rose. "Thank you, sir," said Shelley. "May we see your sketch when it is finished?"

Herr Keffner touched his hat. "Of course. Farewell."

We parted from him and set off along the deck, submerged in our separate thoughts. But when we reached the bow, and turned to go back, I laid my hand on Shelley's arm. "What are you thinking about?"

He drew my hand through the crook of his elbow. "Why, I am thinking about the same things as you. Experiments, noxious potions, a man driven by insanity to desperate actions. How amazed Jane will be when we tell her! Do you think the furniture in her cabin will move, or is furniture on boats nailed to the floor?"

I laughed. "I believe it is. But I was thinking about something quite different. Did you not notice that you referred to me as 'my wife', and did not even remember you were telling an untruth?"

The river breeze lifted the brim of my bonnet and made Shelley's hair flap into his eyes. He pushed it away so that he could look at me. "To me it is not an untruth," he said simply. "You *are* my wife."

I was alone in our cabin. For a long time after the candle burnt itself out I had lain sleepless, watching daylight creep around the edges of the tiny, shuttered window. Shelley, as restless as I was, had gone for a walk on the deck.

The presence of his child inside me was both wondrous and frightening. I placed my palms on my belly and tried to imagine how it would feel to hold the child in my arms, as my own mother had held me for such a short time before she died. My heartbeat quickened. Was I going to die too, when my own baby was born?

What would happen to me if my baby proved my murderer? Would I go to heaven, or hell? For Shelley, of course, neither existed. But he was a man, and could never die in childbirth. Dark thoughts. I pressed my hands to my temples, but there was no escape. My thoughts darkened further. They turned to the alchemist. The pathetic story of his ambition and disappointment played upon my too-ready emotions, and my eyes filled with tears. But I did not weep. I lay there open-eyed, my limbs rigid with the shock of a sudden, unspeakable thought.

Why, since Shelley insisted that it was not God who had fashioned the child I carried, should a modern scientist not make a figure of human dimensions? Then, why should he not infuse it with the spark which would breathe life into its heart?

My brain whirling, I was both fascinated and repelled. Surely, if such a living creature should be created, the experiment would be a lesson to us all in over-reaching ambition. The forces of nature, so much more powerful than those of man, should not be meddled with. The scientist would inevitably discover that if we try to interfere with life, we court that very death we are trying to cheat. He would die insane, like the unfortunate alchemist.

The very thought was enough to bring delirium, but I could not retreat from the idea now it had taken hold of me. If the scientist toiled for many, many years, what, in the end, would he produce? A man, or … something else? A being more hideous than the human brain can fathom, and more powerful than human ingenuity can contain? In short, a monster?

There were shadows in the room I had not seen before. My heart pumped fast. I felt perspiration on my face. Was this the delirium I feared, or fear itself?

The early morning river sounds were beginning. I listened to the swishing and sucking of the water against the bows, and the boatmen calling to one other, and Shelley's voice wishing them good morning in German.

Not a monster; an angel.

My angel. My own, perfect angel. And soon, his perfect child.

Streetwalker or Princess

*W*hat had started out as a glorious adventure ended in poverty and low spirits. Our Channel crossing was stormy. We were all sick. My body convulsed so violently I feared for the precious cargo in my belly. Shelley wrapped me in a blanket and comforted me, though he was unwell himself. Jane lay on our pile of baggage and groaned.

"I wish I had never agreed to come with you!" she cried accusingly. "You have used me ill, both of you. I have suffered fatigue and hunger. Why did you not tell me how little money you had, Shelley? And you, *you*..." Her miserable glance pierced me. "You always hated me."

I had not the energy to argue. And I, too, was miserable. I feared what would greet us when we arrived in England. My infamous elopement would by now be all over London, to the shame of Fanny and Mama and the despair of my poor father. As the ship rolled I lay in the blanket, with Shelley's arms around me, silent, pale and sick. In my imagination I saw Papa's distress. But I was helpless against his hardened heart.

Two days later, when Jane and I rang the doorbell of our parents' house, Mama's face appeared between the lace curtains of the upstairs drawing-room. We heard her shriek. Then the curtains closed.

Nothing happened for a few minutes. Jane looked away from me, tapping her foot on the boot-scraper. I stared at the familiar black door with its brass lion's head knocker.

"They will not let us in," declared Jane. Her impatience had become nervousness. She spun her parasol this way and that. "They will never speak to us again."

Back in this well-known place I resumed my role of bolder, more worldly sister. I gave an exaggerated sigh. "You and I are girls of sixteen, Jane. We have caused our parents pain, but we are still their daughters. They love us, and will forgive us."

"My mama may forgive *me*," retorted Jane, "but your papa will never forgive *you*."

I was perfectly ready to believe these cruel words, but I could not betray this to Jane. "Your fatuousness astonishes me," I told her mercilessly. "My papa's love for my poor mama was as strong as Shelley's for me, and their situation was equally unorthodox. How can he not forgive me?"

"Those facts made no difference at all to Papa's banishment of Shelley from this house, and his fury when we ran away," she reminded me. She stopped spinning her parasol. I felt her hand on my elbow, and turned to meet the look I knew she would be bestowing on me. There it was: arch, triumphant. "It is not *I*, my dear Mary, who holds a fatuous belief!"

The door opened. The housemaid, Anne, bobbed a

bashful curtsy. "Master says Miss Jane is to come up."

"Alone?" enquired Jane, shutting her parasol.

"Yes, Miss."

Jane did not look at me again. She swept past Anne into the hallway and began to climb the stairs.

"Am I not to go upstairs too?" I asked the maid.

She raised troubled eyes to my face. "No, Miss Mary, I believe not."

"Thank you, Anne."

When she had shut the door I pressed my face against the shop window. The shop was empty, though the "Closed" sign was not on the door. I tried the handle. The door was locked.

Trembling with frustration, tinged with the self-pity of one whose secret pessimism has been proved correct, I walked back to the lodgings Shelley had found for us.

He was sitting in a too-small chair, his long legs folded inelegantly beneath him, writing furiously. When I came in he did not look up.

"It is exactly as I said it would be," I announced. "My father will not see me."

He still did not cease from his task, nor did he look at me. His eyes had the glossy look of inspiration flowing faster than the ink. I doubted he even heard my words.

Going into the bedroom, I caught a glimpse of myself in the mirror.

Women in my condition were supposed to look plumper than usual. But I was so thin that when I had dressed to visit Mama and Papa that morning, I had had to tie a sash under my bosom to pull in the excess material of my gown. Women in my condition were supposed to look radiant, and expectant in every sense of the word. But my face looked stricken. Pale, shadowed, bony.

I sank on my knees beside the bed, clutching the bedcovers in my fists, refusing to cry. The truth was, I had been dealt a blow more painful than any physical injury. My beloved father, on whose selfless affection I had depended for my entire motherless life, had banished me from his house.

How alone I felt, kneeling there on that threadbare carpet. Jane had been welcomed back into the arms of her mama. Shelley, lost in poetry, was careless of the fact that the man he had hoped would be his patron was now implacably opposed to him. I would have to face this calamity without his help.

"Mary, what is the matter?" came his voice from the doorway. "Are you unwell?"

"No." I tried to rise, but my foot caught on my gown. "I am quite well."

He helped me from my knees to the bed. He sat down on its edge and embedded his fingers energetically in his hair. "I have been composing," he said.

"Yes, I know."

"I am writing of Prometheus."

"Prometheus?"

"In Greek mythology, the demigod who created mankind out of clay and stole fire from Zeus to enable them to live. I cannot stop thinking about the alchemist Herr Keffner spoke of, who wanted to create a living man. My poem is about the triumph of freedom over oppression, to show that mankind —"

He stopped, his curls still tangled around his hands. He

had at last remembered where I had been. "Where is Jane?" he asked.

I answered with a shrug.

"Was she admitted to your father's house, while you were not?" he asked, horror-struck.

I nodded miserably.

The mattress juddered as Shelley slapped his palms down on it in frustration. After a moment's thought, he jumped up and walked about the room. "Mary," he exclaimed, "the man is a scoundrel! You are better off away from him."

"My father is not a scoundrel," I told him calmly.

He sat down again. "Deluded, then."

"Yes, deluded."

His eyes were pensive, looking at nothing. After a long pause, he said, "Perhaps we should go back to Europe. Perhaps we should never have come home."

There was a weary edge to his voice. My despair began to trickle away, and I embraced him. He responded immediately, as if he had been starved of physical contact for years. He was indeed a child, or an animal. He did what came naturally to him. To his cost, perhaps.

I let him kiss me and put his hands on me as much as he wanted. When he next spoke, his voice was calm again. "This reminds me of that day in the churchyard, when I took you for the first time. The grass stains on my shirt never came out."

"No matter! No one would notice them among all the other stains."

"Why do you scold me so?" he asked.

"Because *someone* has to scold you, or you would be even worse than you are."

He kissed me again. "And do you remember that I told you it was my birthday?"

"Of course. How could I forget? You told me I was giving you a beautiful present." I touched his cheek. "You are a very good seducer."

"Better than you know!" he said mischievously.

"What do you mean?"

He began to laugh. "My real birthday fell some weeks after that day, when we were in Switzerland!"

I stared at him. "And you never told me?"

"It was hardly prudent to do so, was it?" I could hardly make out his words through his laughter. "After you had already given me such a beautiful present for my imaginary birthday! How do you like that for a seducer's trick?"

I did *not* like it. I pushed him away. "It was not a trick, it was a lie! What other lies did you tell me, in order to dishonour me?"

"Dishonour you!" he repeated mockingly. "You did not consider it dishonourable at the time!"

"How do you know what I considered it?"

He stopped laughing. "Mary…" he began, but I would not let him go on.

"You are the father of Harriet's child, are you not?" I asked. "*You*, not her imaginary lover!"

Shelley bowed his head to avoid my gaze. My anger rose. I pushed him again, harder this time. "You see, I have grown up since those days in the churchyard! You are exactly as Papa said!"

His head came up quickly. "What did he say?"

"That you are not an honourable man. I defended you, but I wish I had not."

"Your father can go to the devil."

"The devil you don't believe—"

"Mary, do not persist in taunting me with my beliefs!"

I was bewildered. Why was he so sensitive about beliefs for which he had been prepared to give up his university career and risk his inheritance? Did he not, after all, have the courage of his convictions? Was my lover, like my father, unprepared to put his principles to the test?

"I will not do so again," I agreed. "But I must insist that you do not curse my father. He is not our enemy."

My voice broke on this last word. I could not bear to think of my father as an enemy. And the thought of the pain my elopement had caused him, so invisible to me three months ago, now caused me equal pain.

Shelley's countenance filled instantly with compassion. He tugged me towards him. The ease with which his feelings rushed to his face was one of the things I loved best about him. All resentment, lies and worldweariness dissolved, and we entered our lovers' world again.

"You are my trophy," he murmured. "You are a prize, awarded to the one man worthy of it. And I am that man."

These words delighted me, but I now knew better than to believe Shelley unquestioningly. "A prize!" I said playfully. "Surely you prize me not for myself, but for my father and mother, whose work you profess to admire so much."

"Oh, shocking!" he protested.

"You chose me over Fanny and Jane, did you not, because I am the only daughter whose veins actually contain their mingled blood?"

"Shocking, shocking!"

"Do you deny it?"

"Not at all, you too-intelligent female." He held me very tightly. "I confess, I began with high expectations of the product of this illustrious parentage, but..." He paused, uncertain what to say next.

"But?" I prompted.

"But ... before I had spent five minutes in your company I fell in love with you regardless. You could have been anybody – a streetwalker or a princess. You would still have been my prize."

Claire

*J*ane, for all her accusations on the Channel crossing, could recognize the lesser of two evils. Later that day she returned to our lodgings near the Thames.

"Before you ask," she said, throwing herself into the very chair in which I had found Shelley writing that morning, "I am *not* going back to live with Mama and Papa."

"And Fanny," I added.

Jane gave me a relieved look. "You see, even *you* understand how impossible it is!"

In those cramped rooms, as autumn darkened into winter and the candles had to be lit earlier each day, we three formed an uneasy triangle. Shelley, whose poetic output was great but whose talent as a salesman was not, published little, and we sank daily into further debt. I learned to cook and keep house, as we could not afford a servant. Jane trimmed her bonnets and hems, and dressed her hair, and bemoaned the unfairness of life. To my relief she did not return to her notion that Shelley preferred her. But, as if to confound me, she suddenly began to indulge a different fantasy.

"I no longer wish to be called Jane," she announced one day at the breakfast table.

Shelley and I stared. The obvious question was on my lips, but Jane answered it.

"From this moment everyone will call me Claire. It is my new name."

"Is there a reason for this change?" asked Shelley.

"You will do as I ask, will you not?"

Shelley nodded, and raised his eyebrows in my direction. I did not return his signal. Jane's, or rather Claire's, tendency to self-reinvention was as wearisome to me as it was to him, but in my case was tinged with sisterly indulgence. She was still the child who had played our "The man I marry will…" game. Although I was no longer such a child, I understood.

When Shelley had gone out, and Claire was in her room, I pushed myself to my feet and knocked on her door.

"Come in, Mary!" she called.

She did not rise from her dressing stool. She was putting on her best bonnet.

"Claire…" I began, experimenting with her new name, wondering if she would respond to it.

She turned brightly. "Yes?"

"Where are you going?"

"Shopping."

"May I come with you?"

Turning back, she began to tease out little black curls around her temples. Her face was as smooth and expression-less as a doll's. "Oh, Mary … you walk so slowly these days!" She tied her bonnet-strings and picked up her gloves. "And now I've hurt your feelings!"

"No, you have not." I smiled, to show her I was not

offended. "Will you talk to me awhile, though, before you go?"

She sat down on the bed, looking at me carefully. "Are you unhappy?"

"No," I assured her. "But it is lonely, waiting in this comfortless place, day after day, for the child to be born."

"And of course I *always* want to talk!" she trilled. "How well you know me!"

I *did* know her well. Or perhaps, as the friend and conspirator of her childhood, I knew only Jane. How well would I come to know this bolder, more calculating girl who had rechristened herself Claire?

"Come, sit down," she said with her artless air, patting the bed.

It sagged a little beneath my weight. "The child grows fast," I said ruefully.

"It will be a boy," predicted Claire. "And Harriet will have another girl. *You*, not she, will be the mother of Shelley's son."

"I would like that," I told her.

"It will be so," said Claire, taking my hand. She looked at me with unexpected affection. "After the child is born, my dear Mary, you shall have a new gown. A beautiful one, more beautiful than the one you ruined by soaking it in water. Do you remember that night? What fun we had!"

"It seems long ago."

"A great deal has happened since. But you and I are still those two merry people, are we not?" She gripped my hand tighter. "We have not grown so old and important that we cannot enjoy ourselves, have we?"

"No, indeed."

Smiling meaningfully, she took my other hand. "And we shall be merry again, Mary, I promise you. Merrier than we have ever been, and wealthier, and admired by all. We have escaped from Papa's interminable dinner parties! Do you think that means we may never again have any sport with gentlemen, and laugh ourselves sick when they have gone?"

I withdrew my hands. "I do not understand you."

At that moment we heard the door slam downstairs. Shelley, having taken the stairs three at a time, plunged into Claire's room. He looked sweaty and red-faced; he had been drinking or running, or both.

"I have a son!" he declared triumphantly. "Harriet's child is a boy, born two hours ago!" He was halfway out of the room again. "I have come back to change my coat. I must go to my father-in-law's house immediately. Surely the birth of a grandson will encourage him to dig deep in his pocket!"

Daughter

*C*laire was wrong on two counts. Not only was Harriet's baby a boy, but mine was a girl. She was born in the middle of a cold February night, and bundled so tightly that I could hardly see her little face when she was placed in my arms. I loosened the shawls, and she opened her eyes upon me for the first time.

Oh God, must I remember that moment? No one can know such love until they see their own child. It surged around me like sea water, obliterating all other feeling. I had drowned in love for Shelley; now I was drowning in love for our daughter.

But I was a daughter too. And after that surge of love came another of equal power – the recollection that my own mother had experienced this emotion on the day of my birth, seventeen years ago. I now knew how happy I had made her before she died. The secret, silent guilt that I had murdered her had weighed upon me for years. What could I do to atone?

Fancy plays curious tricks when the brain and body are

exhausted. As I lay there, transfixed by the sight of my baby turning her head, searching for the breast, wanting to suck, wanting to live, the guilt of years began to trickle away. I told myself that fate, destiny, fortune – Shelley would not have allowed me to include God in such a list – had sent this beautiful baby girl as a messenger between my mother's spirit and mine.

Mama, I offer you my child. Her life for your death. And I will bring her up as you would have brought me up. Strong, free, worthy of your love. Worthy of her grandfather's love.

Shelley held the baby and kissed her, declaring her the most beautiful child he had ever beheld. Then he kissed me and thanked me for my labours, and together we looked at our child.

"Your father will not resist the power of his first grandchild," he declared. "Look how she grips my finger! I am confident we shall see him here within the day."

Some hours later I awoke from a dreamless sleep to find Claire standing over me, the baby in her arms. "You have a visitor," she said.

I raised my head from the pillow. "Papa? Is it my Papa?"

"It is not. It is Fanny," she replied, placing the child proudly at my side. "She is impatient to see her niece. I have washed the baby and brushed her hair. Does she not look nice?"

"She does indeed. Thank you, Claire." I squeezed her hand. "Where is Shelley?"

"He has gone to see Harriet and the children," said Claire, arranging my pillows. "He will not be back before evening."

I did not allow this news to wound me. I had become

accustomed to Shelley's manipulation of his relatives. He would use the new baby as a way of extracting money, as he had used the birth of his son a few weeks earlier.

Fanny and I had not met since before my flight to France the previous summer. When she entered the room, her face was full of apprehension. My heart swelled with affection. She had shown both kindness and bravery in coming to see me.

"Come in, come in," I urged her. "Put down that basket and kiss me."

She allowed Claire to take away the basket, brimful with spoils from my stepmother's larder. Then Fanny took off her bonnet, deliberately slowly, it seemed to me, and sat beside the bed. She did not kiss me.

"We are all relieved at home that you are safely delivered," she announced primly. "Our brother Charles sends his affectionate regards."

"I thank him for them," I replied, copying her sombre tone. "And what do Papa and Mama send, apart from a basket of food?"

"Papa sits in the shop, writing, hour after hour. And Mama has been crying ever since we heard the news."

"They will not visit their granddaughter, then?"

"No." She paused, fidgeting with her bonnet-strings, looking down at her lap. Then she seemed to make a decision, and raised her head. "Mary, I do not believe they intend to acknowledge the child. Papa is resolute."

I held the baby tightly, my chin resting on the downy hair that Claire had brushed so carefully. "Thank you, Fanny." Her moral sense was very strong; I knew she had struggled with her conscience. "You were right to tell me."

"I did not know what to do," she confessed. "You and I share a mother. I am of this child's blood." She leant towards me, her hands clasped tightly, her lip quivering. "I feel our mother's spirit in the room. Now, as we speak. Do you not feel it too?"

Fanny had always been a nervous individual, prone to attacks of despair which had tried my stepmother's patience sorely over the years. But I pitied her the joyless existence in the family home I had left. She was not my father's child; neither was she my stepmother's, and her own father was long dead. Apart from our mother's two unmarried sisters, whom Fanny and I had scarcely met, her only true relatives in the world were my baby and myself.

"I felt our mother's presence last night, when I first held my child," I confessed. "She loved us, Fanny. Whatever else happens to us in this world, we can adhere to that truth. She loved us very dearly."

Fanny put her head down. Sobs shook her thin shoulders. She wiped her nose on her glove. "Forgive me," she kept saying. "Forgive me."

"There is no need," I told her. "It is you who have suffered for your forgiveness of *me*. You are the only one who corresponded with us when we were away, and kept us informed about the malicious gossip Harriet Shelley was spreading. It is that gossip, and Mama's outrage, and Papa's obstinacy, which has done such harm. You are blameless."

She was looking at me with gratitude. "Oh, Mary, I wish you could come home!" she said warmly. Then, after a pause, "You are aware, are you not, that all Papa wants you to do is…" She faltered. She could not say it.

"Leave Shelley?" I suggested. "Of course! I shall deliver

him back to his wife and children and appear on Papa's doorstep with my baby in my arms, begging mercy. 'Behold your prodigal daughter!' I shall cry. 'Take me in, and let me work in your shop!' "

Even Fanny, a stranger to gaiety, allowed herself a small smile. "You are not going to do that, are you?" she ventured.

The baby answered for me. She set up a loud wail, alarming her aunt and amusing her mother, and was not quiet again until I had put her to the breast. Fanny studied the tiny mouth working and the tiny fists waving. On her face was an expression of profound sympathy.

"If I could only be loved by a man like Shelley," she said, "I would never leave him either. Truly, love is the only thing that can conquer all evil. Even death itself, as Jesus teaches us."

Fanny's visit assumed great importance in the light of subsequent events. I remember it even now with affection, as the one point of light in the dark world that embraced me only two weeks after my daughter was born.

Love can conquer evil, she had said. But what kind of love could possibly conquer the evil which befell us so suddenly, and snatched away our happiness? How, after the release from guilt which the baby's birth had brought me, could I bear to be thrown into that prison again?

One night I laid the child down in her cradle before I went to bed. Shelley was sleeping in the drawing-room. The baby lay on her back, her head to one side, her fist denting her cheek in peaceful sleep. Instinct woke me a few hours later, at the hour she usually needed feeding. She was not crying.

I got out of bed and went to the cradle. She was still in the same position as when I had left her, so deeply asleep I was reluctant to wake her. It was when I slid my hands under her body to lift her that I felt my heart explode with shock. She was not asleep. The dent in her cheek made by her fist did not disappear when her hand was moved. She was quite, quite cold.

Summoned by my screams, Shelley and Claire rushed into the room. I remember the sound of their raised voices, and Shelley clasping the baby to his breast, his face convulsed. I remember Claire's insistence that we call a physician and an undertaker, despite my pleas to have the small cold body beside me for the rest of the night. I remember Shelley, in the end, agreeing with her, and strangers coming up the stairs. After that I remember only darkness and muddle.

"Send for Fanny, send for Fanny!" someone's voice urged.

But Fanny did not come. I learnt afterwards that Claire had written to her, pleading with her to comfort her sister at such a time. But no reply was received, and although Claire watched for her day after day, Fanny did not appear.

People, places and events distorted themselves in my feverish brain. I told myself that Fanny could not bear to enter the house where the baby with whom she had expressed such a profound connection had died. I begged my dead mother to forgive me for not being able to keep my baby from the same fate which had befallen her. I imagined them together in heaven, my child as she was when I had seen her lying in her cradle for the last time, my mother as she looked in the only portrait my father had of her. Stiffly-corseted, severe.

I felt I had lost my mother, my sister and my daughter because I had not deserved to keep them. They had been taken away as a punishment far greater than my father's hard-heartedness. But *why*, when I had never wished anyone harm?

Driven by grief, my rebelliousness rose.

"Let us go back to Europe! Please, Shelley!" I implored. "Claire is wild to go. She says she cannot stay in England a moment longer, with people gawping at her as if she were a bear on a chain."

Shelley's eyes brightened. "Switzerland?"

"The bear on a chain did not like Switzerland very much," I replied. "And I thought *you* wanted to be near the sea."

"And you, my darling? What is your desire?"

"I do not care where I go, as long as it is away from here," I told him. "I will not stay to hear society's cruel comments about the death of our precious child. Cannot you imagine the gossips, whispering behind their fans? 'They have got what they deserve,' they will say."

Shelley nodded mischievously. "'And he still keeps that forlorn little wife and two children!'" he declared in a high, disapproving voice. "'My dear, the man is a monster!' You are right, Mary. We *shall* go abroad again."

George

 $\mathcal{W}$e did not go abroad immediately, though.

To my joy, I discovered I was expecting another child very soon after our daughter's death, and did not wish to have the baby in Switzerland. It would be wintertime anyway. We decided to wait till the following spring.

This second child was a boy. Not, alas, Shelley's first son, but a beautiful healthy baby nonetheless. Optimistically we called him William, my father's name.

I never left him in a cradle. He slept in our bed with us, and I watched over him every minute of the day. As the days lengthened and warmed, and the baby thrived, our contentment was increased by the sale of several of Shelley's poems for publication. His reputation was growing daily; favourable reviews abounded. Intellectuals of radical persuasion admired him, and their company fired his interest in politics. He increased his fame both as a poet and a campaigner for social justice by defending in his writing the causes of those oppressed by despotism or political corruption. My admiration grew too. I had fulfilled my girlish ambition to find a clever man.

If only my father had extended forgiveness, my happiness would have been complete.

Sitting in our cramped parlour, I tried to write. The notion of a story lay in the recesses of my brain, fashioned from our encounter with Herr Keffner. But I did not feel free either to indulge my imagination or improve my skill without my ever-supportive critic, my father.

I read and reread the books my parents had written. Nowhere in them did I find condemnation of the idealistic love Shelley and I had found. There was only praise for its liberating influence.

Why could my father not see that a man of Shelley's gifts could not become a poet under ordinary circumstances? A poet was a prophet, a genius, a visionary. His admirers understood, as my father did not, that a creative spirit such as Shelley's needed to live a different existence, an experimental existence in a household freed from society's bonds. And Shelley loved me because I, too, was unshackled. Why, then, was I so cruelly punished by my papa, whose teachings had first unlocked those shackles?

"Do not spoil your beauty with self-pity," Shelley counselled me one evening, when I had been crying. "I will help you with your writing far better than he. And anyway, he is causing more unhappiness to himself than to you."

"Why do you say that?"

He sighed. "I passed him in the street this very morning."

"And?"

"He cut me. Quite dead."

"Oh, Shelley!"

"But do you not see that he has wrought his own misery?

Can you imagine what living in that house with your step-mother and Miss Melancholy must be like, now you and Claire are no longer there?"

It was true. The house must have been very quiet without the shrieks and giggles with which Claire and I had disturbed Papa's peace. And there must have been more room, too, without our gowns and shoes and bonnets and cloaks and all the paraphernalia of girlhood – bundled letters, scrapbooks and more pieces of abandoned embroidery than Mama would ever find.

There was no doubt that from the day Shelley had walked into the shop and demanded a sovereign, nothing had been as it was. He had brought love and adventure, and given me the rare gift of knowing I was admired by a man who was himself admired by many. But he had taken things away too. Elusive things. Things which drifted around my head like half-remembered dreams: childhood conspiracies, sisterly loyalty, my father's devoted respect for *all* his daughters.

"Do you know Lord Byron?" Claire enquired of Shelley casually one morning.

"Lord Byron?" exclaimed Shelley. His voice became fervent. "Who does *not* know Lord Byron? He is a great poet, a man noble in name and in genius. You have read his work, of course?"

"Of course," agreed Claire, unmoved by this extravagant praise. "So you have never met him, then?"

"No."

"Did you know that he has connections with the theatre?" asked Claire. "How I long to meet someone who may procure me an entry to that wonderful world!"

Claire's appetite for wealth and notoriety had been whetted by the scandal Shelley and I had caused. As our notoriety grew, so did hers by association. She agreed that we should go abroad again in order to escape gossip, but she also revelled in the knowledge that people were talking about her.

She longed, truly, to be famous. Her desire for attention had always been indulged at home, and sensational novels had fed her imagination. Because she could play the piano and sing a little, she had a notion of herself as a performer. She was merely awaiting the moment when her appearance on the London stage would make her the darling of the wealthy and the envy of the poor. She would be adored by men and disapproved of by their wives. She could see it all, and had frequently described it to me.

"Indeed!" I exclaimed. Lord Byron's scandalous way of living was as widely known and disapproved of as Shelley's. "And did *you* know he is estranged from his wife and is living in sin with his sister-in-law?"

"What gossips women are!" cried Shelley. "And what, pray, is 'living in sin', if it is not exactly what *we* are doing?"

I stared at him. "Oh! But it does not *feel* sinful to us, does it?"

He grinned. "I will tell you something about Lord Byron," he said mischievously. "He has a villa on the shores of Lake Geneva. If we make ourselves known to him, I see no reason for him not to welcome us there, do you?"

"Oh, Shelley!" exclaimed Claire. "Let *me* be the one to make myself known to him! I have heard so much about him – and not just gossip, Mary – I can hardly contain my desire to meet him. Do you know where his London residence is, Shelley?"

"I do," he said. "By all means be our ambassador, my dear Claire, if you wish."

Later, Shelley watched Claire from the window of the lodgings as she set off on her quest to conquer Lord Byron. "I will wager that she succeeds," he muttered. "Byron will be charmed, poor devil."

"He would not like to be described so, to be sure!" I observed.

I did not add that knowing Claire as I did, I assumed her intentions towards Lord Byron included becoming his lover, notwithstanding the estranged wife and alleged mistress. She would make the same assault on him as she had made on Shelley. The difference was, of course, that I was not there to prick her conscience and, from what I had heard, Byron had no conscience at all.

Hours later, Claire returned. "Imagine, Mary!" she instructed me breathlessly. "Lord Byron – he allowed me to call him George, and is very, very charming – devoted the entire afternoon to me! And he intends to spend the summer in Switzerland! I believe it is only a matter of time before we receive an invitation to join him there! How splendid it will be!"

I was not so certain. "Are you sure?"

"Oh, Mary…"

"Does he truly want the whole troop of us to invade his household?"

She stamped her foot impatiently. "You always used to accuse *me* of not being romantic enough! Why, it was the thing I loved about you, the way you pursued love and freedom, and never cared what people thought! Do you not remember how you stood up to Papa that day in the drawing-room, when I brought Shelley's letter? Where has your courage gone?"

Her words stung me. I did not know where my courage had gone. "Please, consider Lord Byron's —"

"Oh, do call him George!" she urged. "He is the dearest, sweetest, most amiable man. When you meet him you will fall in love with him just as I have done. But mind he does not fall in love with you!"

Ignoring the coy look which accompanied this, I persisted. "Claire, I beg you to consider. Do you not understand that 'George' is simply not interested in me, or you? It is *Shelley* he wants."

"Shelley? *Shelley?*" she repeated, with the sort of frown she used to give me when I suggested going for a walk on a rainy day, or eating no bonbons after dinner. It meant "You are mad and I pity you".

"What nonsense you talk, Mary! Why should he care about *Shelley?*"

"Because Shelley is a sought-after poet these days, and poets always seek each other's society."

"Ach!" she exclaimed impatiently, tossing her head in exact imitation of her mother.

"And furthermore," I continued, unflinching, "Lord Byron is doubtless attracted by Shelley's style of living and political beliefs, which are similar to his own. If he invites us at all, he will do so in order to welcome *Shelley* to his villa, and display *him*, not us, to his influential guests."

If Claire had not been Claire, she would have received this message clearly. But she was incapable of this degree of understanding: in her world, only *she* was attractive, only *she* was irresistible.

"But the invitation will be to *me*, Mary," she insisted. "Have you not listened to anything I have said?"

I sighed. It was no use. "Will you help me fold William's napkins?" I asked. "The nurse has toothache and I have sent her to bed."

Our party in Switzerland consisted of Shelley, Claire, myself and baby William. The nurse remained in England with her toothache. George had rented the Villa Diodati, the most impressive villa on Lake Geneva, positioned to command the most arresting prospect. And as I had predicted, we did not receive an invitation to stay with him there.

The less grand house Shelley had taken for us, however, was to my mind more charming. Unlike George's villa it had no fluted pillars or marble floors. But it had pleasant south-facing rooms, with long windows overlooking gardens where William could play safely.

"How exciting!" Claire giggled as we unpacked. "George will come tomorrow!"

Claire's capacity for self-delusion had already propelled her into a reckless affair with an unscrupulous man. I was strongly convinced that Lord Byron did not return my sister's affection, but, inspired by his fast and furious poetry and his equally fast and furious way of life, she could not resist her fantasy.

At last I understood what she had meant when she had outlined our future life of merriment and ease, and new dresses. She had grown tired of her role as the superfluous member of a two-woman-one-man triangle. Defeated in her attempts to prise Shelley from my side, she had been plotting for many months a strategy for getting her *own* poet, her *own* aristocrat. And most important of all she wanted her *own* source of scandal and notoriety, greater even than Shelley could boast.

George duly arrived in a carriage and six with one guest and a large retinue of servants, and set up house in the Villa Diodati. But he did not call.

"Does he expect us to call on *him*?" I asked Shelley. "I am not sure of the etiquette."

"Etiquette be damned," declared Shelley.

"But he is our social superior, is he not?"

"Social superior be damned," said Shelley. "Let him come when he likes."

Claire could scarcely contain herself. I was reminded of the feverish days between my meeting with Shelley in the bookshop and his first afternoon call, when I had gazed perpetually out of the front windows, elated and despairing by turns. Claire sat on the balcony outside her room, from where she could see the roof and some of the windows of the Villa Diodati, all day for several days, until impatience overcame her and she dashed off a letter to George.

I did not see its contents, but I could imagine her pleadings. Her chance to parade her conquest before the world, which his scandalous lifestyle did not allow at home in London, was too precious to miss. And the summer was passing.

Then, when more than a week had gone by and Claire had stopped sitting on the balcony, he appeared. It was the early evening of a scorching day. Shelley was outside by the lake when Claire and I, who were preparing supper, heard a commotion and an aristocratic English voice. I gathered William into my arms and followed Claire's shrieking, fluttering figure down the front steps to the beach.

We stared at the unexpected sight that met us. Her lover and mine were splashing barefoot in the shallows, hauling in a rowing boat and shouting instructions to each other like fishermen. George, who had jumped out of the boat when he saw Shelley on the shore, was soaked to his waist, and wore his shirt tied up, more like a Swiss peasant than a member of the English ruling class. Shelley, helpless with laughter, lost his footing, sat down hard on the pebbles and laughed louder.

"Have you never handled a boat before, man?" roared George. "And you call yourself an Englishman?"

"An Englishman would arrive on a proper sailing boat with a proper crew!" called Claire, advancing down the beach. "Not row himself like any common oarsman!"

Shelley tugged the boat with all his strength, and at last he and George succeeded in beaching it. George collapsed at Claire's feet and caught the hem of her skirt in his teeth. Shelley lay beside him, holding his stomach and groaning.

"What are you doing, George? Are you being a dog? Is this a game?" asked poor Claire.

George released her dress and growled. Shelley groaned louder. Their combined noise was louder and more childish than anything William could produce.

"Let the dog kiss his mistress!" exclaimed George, and before Claire knew what was happening he had pulled her down on her back, put one leg over both hers, wet breeches and all, and bestowed a passionate kiss on her lips. Understandably, as soon as she could breathe she began to scream.

If I picture George now as he was when I first saw him,

my impression is of something not entirely human. Not devilish, exactly, but otherworldly, as if he were merely borrowing time on earth, and must return to some immortal abode. Physically, he was tall like Shelley, but burlier, and older than I had expected. He had a slight limp from a malformed foot, but his air of eager charm was so engaging, this deficiency went almost unnoticed. He might have been eighteen, like Claire and me.

The pretty Swiss nursemaid we had engaged came out of the house, shading her eyes against the lowering sun.

"Elise!" I called, and she approached, holding out her arms for the child. "Will you take William to bed?"

George had got up. "My dear Mrs Shelley, what a delightful domestic scene!"

He looked very tall, with the evening light stretching his shadow along the beach. Hauling Claire to her feet, he advanced towards me with one arm around her shoulders and the other in a mock salute. "And Master Shelley too!" he exclaimed. "I am a mightily privileged fellow, am I not, to be welcomed by such famous personages!"

I was amused at the heavy-handed irony of "Mrs Shelley". He knew very well I was not married. "But surely *you* are the personage whose reputation goes before him, Lord Byron," I said.

He let Claire go and bent towards Elise and me in an elegant bow. William reached out his dimpled fist and made an exploration of George's dark, damp hair. As I pulled the child's hand away, George took my own and kissed it. "I wish I could believe so, madam," he said gravely. "But Shelley's star is rising faster than mine."

Hearing his name, Shelley made his way up the beach.

He was no longer laughing, but his face had the abandoned expression it wore when he was at his most delighted with life. I gave William to Elise, who held him up for his father's kiss. As she took the child into the house, I entwined my arm with Shelley's, and he rested his cheek against my temple. He smelt as salty and sweaty as, in Claire's words, a common oarsman.

"I love you," I said to him matter-of-factly, as if I were indeed addressing a servant. "Never forget how much I love you, whatever happens to us."

He raised his head and looked down at me. A dazed look came into his beautiful eyes. "But you like George too, do you not?" he asked.

It was still dark. No brilliant Swiss morning outlined the black of the shutters. Even without feeling the mattress beside me I knew I was alone.

"Where are you?" I called.

A candle flickered in the passageway. Shelley stood in the doorway, his gigantic shadow leaping onto the wall. The flame was weak, and threw only enough light under his chin to reveal his neck and shoulders. He looked unearthly, like a being who had rejected life and welcomed the grave. He seemed halfway between here and heaven. His eyes were in shadow; I could not see their expression.

"Are you ill?" I asked, fighting panic.

"No, only sleepless. Go back to sleep."

"Have you taken anything?" I persisted. He had, I knew.

"No. Do not alarm yourself. I will come back to bed soon. Now leave me alone."

He reached for the door handle. As he lunged forward I saw his shirt billow in the candlelight, like a sail, his thin body the mast. Then he closed the door, and the room was in darkness once more.

In the Company of Spirits

We found that George's guest was his friend Polidori, a young part-Italian doctor who innocently admired everything he saw, and never succeeded in working out my relationship to either Shelley or Claire. He immediately conceived an infatuation with me, a situation which George found hilarious and did his best to encourage.

The two men, surrounded by luxury and pampered by George's huge staff, seemed bent on spending as much money as possible in the shortest time possible during their stay. In my heart I disapproved, but the beauty of our surroundings seduced us all.

By day or night, the sky, the lake and the mountains presented an array of changing colours and textures. The air was sweet, the prospect delightful, the company congenial. We went to the Villa Diodati every day, formally dressed at first, then gradually less and less so, bearing picnic baskets and fishing-rods and the box containing William's clothes and toys. It was pleasant to idle away the time on or off shore, playing and sleeping, drinking from George's inexhaustible wine cellar, and talking, always talking.

George's mental facility was extraordinary. I could see why Shelley admired him so. It was his ability to dash from one complex subject to another, without apparently needing time to breathe, which gave the impression of sprite-like powers. His listeners' ears were bombarded with wit, while their eyes devoured a countenance not quite angelic – that description must always be reserved for Shelley – but certainly heavenly in some more mysterious way.

He and Shelley shared many things. They were both publicly recognized poets, though George's fame was the greater. Both had incurred the disapproval of their noble families and retreated to Europe to escape scandal. George's passion for wild mountain scenery was as great as Shelley's. And it had been clear from their first meeting that boating would become their favourite occupation.

Shelley had often professed to crave the wildness of the sea, but in landlocked Switzerland he seemed willing to forgo it in favour of rowing or sailing up and down Lake Geneva in all weathers. Neither he nor George ever having received much instruction in the art of sailing, they spent many hours adrift, the sails furled, the oars idle, writing, laughing, talking, and talking more.

And during that summer, as we walked and talked and ate and drank together, we discovered another, perhaps less worthy, mutual passion. When Shelley and I told George of our encounter with the story of the mad alchemist, he stopped in the act of trying to get William to swallow a tumbler of wine and stared at us with saucer eyes and an open mouth.

"Madness! Bloody murder! Lonely castles!" he cried. "In

my opinion, all novels should contain nothing else!"

"Oh, George, how right you are!" replied Claire, hanging on his arm. "And how I long for a new horror story! I have read *The Castle of Otranto* five times." She turned to the company. "Do you think writers are truly aware of the public's demand for murder and revenge? And abduction? Abduction is my favourite!"

"Of course they are, but they cannot supply such novels quickly enough to satisfy the readers' bloodlust," observed Shelley "My dear Claire, why not write one yourself?"

A gleam came into her eyes. She was seeing herself at her writing-desk, a light shawl draped around her shoulders, frowning daintily in concentration over her masterpiece. "I may well do that, Shelley, so do not jest!" she said.

George, whose absorbent brain and tireless enthusiasm were well suited to such ideas, offered his own accounts of experiments he had read of. Shelley, tormented as ever by the question of God's monopoly on life-creation, sat up late, scribbling remnants of their conversations down so that he could use them in future defence of his atheism.

"George calls the creation of life 'the place where science meets the supernatural'," he told me, impressed. "I wish I had thought of such an apt phrase."

For my part, I was not so much frightened by the alchemist's ambition as interested. I did not tell Shelley and George about the lonely, feverish dawn I had spent before my daughter's birth, when the scientific and moral implications of tampering with death had played so forcibly on my mind. But I joined their discussions of the subject very readily. If base metal could be turned to gold – and who was to say the secret of alchemy would never be discovered – why could mankind not dream of restoring a lifeless corpse to animation?

Switzerland's summer displayed dramatic elements that year. There were many sunny, calm days, but we also saw rain, strong winds, racing skies and shafts of sunlight piercing the grey clouds, glancing off the waters of the lake like daggers. There were beautiful rainbows. Then more rain, more thunder, more electricity in the sky. My letters to Fanny described ferocious storms that whipped the waters of Lake Geneva into fury, blackening the sky and patterning it with lightning bolts.

One June evening Shelley, Claire and I left William with Elise and set out on our customary after-dinner walk along the shore to the Villa Diodati. It had been a hot, airless day. Claire and I wore no shawls.

"We shall have a mighty storm tonight," predicted Shelley.

"Good!" Claire was always enthusiastic about storms.

"You only hope for a storm because it will provide you with an excuse to stay the night with George," I remarked.

"My dear sister, you are mistaken," said Claire coldly, though we both know I was not.

"I wonder how Mr Polidori's ankle fares," I said.

Three days ago George had encouraged his friend to make the reckless leap from the balcony of the Villa Diodati in order to help me, the object of his unspoken desire, up the steep path to the door.

"I wish it better," said Shelley. "Temporary insanity must have caused him to sprain his ankle in such circumstances."

"I have heard *love* called temporary insanity," said Claire, with a meaningful look at me.

George and Polidori, who had evidently enjoyed a hearty dinner and a great deal of wine, were sitting in the drawing-room, smoking and attempting to play cards when we arrived. George rose to greet us, but Polidori remained sitting by the empty grate, his heavily bandaged foot propped up on a footstool.

"My friend's injury still prevents him from walking, as you see," explained George. "We are prisoners in our castle." He grasped our hands as warmly as if he had not seen us for years. "I cannot tell you how welcome you all are!"

He patted Polidori on the shoulder. "Come on, man!" he encouraged. "Tell the ladies how your foot is going on. Ladies like nothing better than to hear of ailments."

Shelley commandeered the cards and dealt anew. Claire and I sat down. The room was shady and very still. A bashful Polidori told, haltingly, of how he could still put no weight on the sprain, and of George's insistence that they call for a physician the next day.

I hardly listened. The air oppressed me; the perspiration on my skin would not evaporate; my hair stuck to my scalp. I wished I was safe at home with William and Elise. I did not want to walk back through the rain, but nor did I want to spend the night in this palatial but cheerless house. I wished we had not come.

"How dark it gets!" observed Polidori, glad to steer the subject away from his embarrassing ankle. His large, rather feminine eyes alighted on me. "But do not fear, ladies, the gentlemen will not allow any harm to come to you."

"Pray, Mr Polidori, what good are men against such whims of nature?" asked Claire briskly. "If the storm wishes to blow the house down it will do so without intervention from anybody."

"Who else is playing cards?" asked Shelley. "Claire?"

"I do not think so." She went to the long windows, which overlooked the lake. "I feel out of sorts tonight."

I did not sit down at the card table either. I had no wish to talk to Polidori, so I joined Claire at the window. I put my arm around her shoulders. Her bare upper arm felt sticky with the heat. Side by side, separated by our thoughts, we regarded the prospect from the window.

The lake reflected the setting sun's last rays as keenly as a sword flashing in the sunlight. Watching the water, I was struck again by the strength of the light from heaven. Far, far brighter than any light man could produce, the power it contained was truly unassailable. What might happen if such power should ever come into the hands of men?

The last gleam of the sun vanished below the horizon. The storm was gathering: clouds rushed in from the west, the wind gusted in the increasing gloom. Along the shore the trees flailed their branches like ghostly dancers. Above the heaving water the clouds looked low enough for us to reach out of the window and touch them.

"How black the sky becomes!" I exclaimed. "See, Claire, how magnificent the mountains look against such a background! That one could be a giant sleeping, could it not? And that one a huge creature of the deep, unnaturally still and quiet?"

"A creature?" said Claire. "What sort of creature?"

As we watched, a fork of white lightning tore the sky. Then another, and another, flickering, flashing, chasing each other as if alive. Then a boom of thunder, loud enough to make us all cover our ears, broke over the house. Screaming with a mixture of delight and terror, Claire put her hands over her face, turned blindly and stumbled into the room.

Shelley, as ready as ever to indulge her, led her to a chair. "You had better come away from the window, my dear," he advised. "Then the creature will gobble up Mary first, and leave you alone."

He and Polidori were laughing. Polidori, who was recovering from his own obvious fear of the storm, slapped his thigh and declared, twice or three times, what a good joke it was.

"You are cruel!" Claire said accusingly. "I believe you all prey upon my nervous disposition deliberately!"

I paid her no heed. In the brooding silence of that half-dark room, my imagination had soared. The sunset's vital beams, and the power contained in the lightning flash, had inspired me.

"Shelley…" I laid my hand on his arm. "Do you not think that the alchemist, experimenting in his castle, might have tried to raise life in dead flesh by the use, perhaps, of electricity?"

He stared at me. "What can you be thinking of? He lived over one hundred years ago. The notion of electricity is a modern one."

"May we speak of something else?" asked Claire plaintively.

"Electricity *is* a modern notion, that is true," I persisted. "But we have not yet harnessed it, and put it to use. Who is to say that the alchemist did not have the *notion* too?"

George was still sitting in his chair at the card table. He looked at me intently, but his words were for Shelley.

"My dear Shelley," he said, amiably but with purpose, "it is very interesting that a young and beautiful woman should propose such a thing."

Shelley's face took on the affectionate expression it wore whenever he heard praise of me. "Mary may be young and beautiful, George, but that is not all she is!"

George had not taken his eyes from my face. "What have you heard about the uses of electricity?" he asked me.

"I have heard nothing."

Truly, I could not tell where the suggestion had come from. I hesitated, looking for reassurance to Shelley, who merely raised his eyebrows. "I have seen lightning in the sky, as has everyone," I continued. "And I have often wondered, also like everyone else, what makes life? What is the meaning of the Creation?"

All the men, and Claire, were listening. I gathered my wits. "Is it … could it possibly be in the gift of mankind to bestow life on inanimate objects? And if life really is a 'spark' of some kind, who is to say that spark will not come from electricity, if only we had the knowledge to bend it to our will?"

George was still watching me. Boldly I looked back at him. Despite his superiority of title, wealth, sex and age, the words of an eighteen-year-old girl in a sprigged cotton dress had impressed him.

"I have a better idea than cards," he said.

His gaze – penetrating, intelligent, accustomed to his own superiority – never left my face. None of us spoke. George sat forward in his chair. "Shall we all follow Mary's excellent example," he suggested, "and spend this evening in the company of spirits?"

"Capital idea!" exclaimed Polidori. Then, with a frown, "But what do you actually mean, George?"

"I mean ghost stories," said George. "Let us each tell one, here in the darkness, with the storm raging outside."

My heart was on fire. Many things I had not understood before had linked themselves effortlessly together. Nightmarish visions, dreams that had dogged me day and night for years. The power and glory of the storm. The idea that a scientist might make a creature more monstrous than any God has devised. The earth-shattering possibility that life itself could lie in the ferocity of those sky-sparks which even now crackled their way across the heavens.

No one spoke. I sat down beside Claire. Lightning again illuminated the room; for a swift moment her face became a round, white mask. Thunder grumbled, further away.

"Come, George," I said. "Will you not be the first to tell us a spine-chilling tale?"

"No indeed, Mistress Mary," he replied. "I wish to hear one from *you*. We all want to be witness to your far-reaching imagination."

I took a bottle from the wine-cooler on the table. "I would far rather hear a tale from the imagination of a true poetic genius than from my own," I insisted. "And so would Mr Polidori." I poured more wine into Polidori's glass. "Would you not, Mr Polidori?"

Polidori blushed. "My dear Mrs Shelley, whatever you say." He raised his full glass to the company, spilling some wine on his breeches as he did so. "Let George begin the storytelling. Indeed, I am content to listen, and be bewitched!"

George did not question his friend's election of him as performer. But as I filled his glass he made one last attempt to persuade me. "I know you have a story to tell," he said, his eyes searching mine. "And, like the ancient mariner, one day you will feel compelled to tell it."

I bowed my head and said nothing.

The only sound was of the wind in the chimneys. Shelley made himself comfortable on the sofa beside me. Claire, looking for intimacy, sat on a cushion at George's feet. I glanced at Polidori. His eyes, reflecting the candlelight, looked like mirrors in his pale face. George leant forward in his chair, the firelight flooding his face, and began to speak.

How potent the imagination can be when circumstance and location combine to nourish it and make it strong! George's gift for the dramatic, so evident in his poetry and in his life, spellbound his listeners tightly. We could not escape. The events of the story were as chilling as Claire could have wished: the spirit of a medieval knight who had been walled up alive in a remote castle was unable to rest until it had slaughtered a virgin. It stalked the beautiful heroine while her lover and would-be rescuer lay wrongly imprisoned in the castle dungeon. Slowly, slowly, the terrible, armoured apparition climbed the spiral staircase to the rooftop whence the girl had fled. Slowly, slowly, George's voice lingered on the horrifying detail – the perspiration on the maiden's brow, her exhaustion, her desperation. And all the time, the knight's footsteps…

The words became an incantation, a pulse as physical as the blood in our veins. Their strange music resounded in that firelit room like the murmuring of something beyond our understanding. Like apparitions, the tragic characters rose from the page and hovered in the air. On and on he went. And as the tale quickened to its climax I felt Shelley clutch my gown, then my arm, then my shoulder, as if to keep a hold on reality. I looked at his face. Fear took hold of me.

"Shelley my dear, what is the matter?"

A terrified scream rose in his breast. He struggled from his seat and lunged towards George, knocking the glass from his hand. The blood-coloured wine stained my dress, George's shirt and the sofa cushion. "Stop!" he shrieked. "Stop, I tell you!"

"Shelley, Shelley, my darling!" I stumbled towards him and pulled him away. As my arms enclosed him I felt assailed by the familiar emotions the touch of his flesh always gave me: love, jealousy, anxiety, exhilaration, delight. "Be calm, my love," I urged. "It is only a story. It is not real. "

"It is the sound of the dead!" he cried. "Their poor corpses have been cut up for experiments, for a madman to try to make them live again! I feel their presence. They are all around the room! Can you not see them?"

"Shelley, Shelley…" murmured George.

For the first time in our acquaintance, I saw George not in control of his countenance. Having not seen this madness before he was shaken to his bones by Shelley's looks and words. "I pray you," he begged his friend, "lie down and drink some water, and let us look after you. You are not well."

Shelley had sunk to his knees. He was sweating, and trembling as if in a fever. Claire, who had scrambled off her cushion and retreated to the shadows at the edge of the room, stared. Polidori's eyes were larger than ever. Immobilized by his injured ankle he looked repeatedly at the door, as if willing help to arrive and carry him away.

I found some of the courage Claire had recently accused me of losing. I stood beside Shelley and looked round the room. "Leave it to me!" I commanded. "I have seen him like this before. And," I added, my voice breaking, "I am partly to blame. I should not have spoken my thoughts aloud."

It was true. The heaving water, the fire in the sky, the demons which stalked my memory – these had all contributed to Shelley's nervous collapse as much as the power of the story and his own unceasing anxiety.

I knelt beside him, but he would not let me touch him. "Look, how they whirl around the room!" he insisted, flailing his arm at the ceiling so suddenly that it almost struck my face.

I looked up. Around the walls was a marble frieze. Shelley may believe in his distraction that it contained the figures of the dead, but the strange thought came to me that George, Claire and Polidori, frozen by horror in the eerie light, resembled the marble carvings themselves. I longed for daylight and fresh air. I longed once more to run away from the unremitting oppression of the Villa Diodati, and hold my son in my arms.

"It is a dream, a mere dream," said George. He was trying to soothe Shelley, but in his voice I heard the edge of hysteria. For all his enthusiasm for the "company of spirits" he saw that Shelley's mind had succumbed to real terror, and he was frightened.

I strove to recover my composure. "Yes, it is dream," I assured Shelley. "You shall be well, my darling. Let me take you home. You must sleep. Sleep will restore you."

We did not go home. George sent for a physician, who gave Shelley a sedative and ordered that he be put to bed. Claire and I fell, exhausted, into a shared bed, since George was in no mood to be amorous. I do not recollect whether it was she or I who wept more that night. But each time I closed my eyes, the sight of my angel and master kneeling on the stone floor, fighting for his reason, rose in my memory. And it will stay there until I die, as indelible as the wine stain on my dress.

Folly and Cruelty

$\mathcal{F}$or three days after the night of the storm Shelley lay in a stupor at the Villa Diodati. When he awoke he was more melancholy than I had ever known him. His consumption of wine, already large due to George's generosity, increased, and he continued to take sleeping-draughts in large doses. Some months earlier he had forsworn the consumption of meat or fish, and existed on a diet of greens, bread and olive oil. His skin, always pale, took on a translucent appearance. He looked more like an angel – or a Renaissance artist's vision of an angel – than ever.

On Shelley's return to our villa, George did not visit him. Handsome, amiable George was preoccupied with his own affairs, and ignored us all – even Claire, whom I suspected to be carrying George's child. I was disappointed but not surprised. I admired George's charm and easy manners, and the way he controlled Claire's melodramatics, but I did not like him. I was sure he would betray Claire if some greater prize presented herself.

"Claire is with child, is she not?" I said to Shelley

eventually, after waiting in vain to be told. "You must have forgotten that I am a mother myself if you think I do not recognize the signs."

He adjusted his pillows – he had not yet risen from the sofa. "If you know, why are you asking me? Are you shocked that Claire has tried to trap George in the time-honoured way?"

"No, I am not shocked," I replied coldly. "Neither by Claire's folly nor by George's cruelty."

"Poor George," he sighed.

"Poor *George*!"

"I merely point out that George is not a man to settle down to family life. He will not see Claire or her child as an impediment to his freedom."

He poured a glass of wine, sipped it, and grimaced. "My thoughts are as bitter as this vile draught. I cannot stop thinking of Harriet, and my two children whom nobody will let me see. It is pitiful, do you not think, that a man should pay so dearly for the mistakes of his youth?"

"Very pitiful," I agreed. "Shall I make you a pen, so that you may write down such a pathetic thought before it is lost in drunkenness?"

He took another sip. "I cannot speak to you when you are in such a humour. Please go away. I must rest."

And with that he replaced the wine glass on the table and turned his face away from me, as petulant as a child.

I went into the kitchen and paced up and down for a few minutes. Then, my agitation subsiding, I wandered into the garden where Elise was playing with William. He was in the almost-crawling stage of babyhood. The nursemaid, in a dirty apron and a straw hat with a torn brim, sat beside him on the grass, righting him whenever he collapsed. I sat down on an iron garden chair to watch this pleasant scene.

In my pocket was a letter. The usual kind of letter, from the usual person. I took it out and reread it.

Why, Mary, Fanny implored, *do you and Claire not abandon your poet-lovers and return to our father's household with William? Do you not realize the shame Mama and Papa are enduring? London society is now not only alive with gossip about you and Shelley, but Claire and Lord Byron also. They are saying that Byron cannot marry her any more than Shelley can marry you. So why do you persist in a lifestyle that will only end in ruin?*

I put the letter away, looking out towards the lake and thinking. The Fanny who had conversed with me so intimately after the birth of my daughter seemed lost beyond recovery now. Claire could not tolerate her stepsister, and often said so. But although my patience was tried, I grieved for Fanny's unhappiness and wished I could atone.

"Might we buy Fanny something?" I asked Claire, who came out of the house just then bearing cushions and a book. "As a souvenir of Switzerland, since she cannot be here with us?"

"A cuckoo clock!" she suggested, with an unkind little laugh. "An irritating gift for an irritating sister!"

I did not wish to quarrel with Claire, but had to defend Fanny. "Yes, she can be irritating, but have some compassion, Claire. She suffers from … she is troubled by melancholy."

I did not add that I sometimes felt the same. Melancholy was ingrained in my nature as well as in Fanny's. It was a bequest from our mother, my father always said. It threatened me now, at the thought of Shelley's distraction and unkindness, my estrangement from my father and Fanny's scoldings, but I concealed it.

"I meant something like a watch, perhaps," I said. "Swiss watches are very fine."

Claire gave me a suspicious look as she arranged her cushions against the sun-bleached wall of the villa. "Indeed they are." She sat down and opened her novel. "Fine enough to be put away in a drawer and never worn!"

"Oh, Claire…" I felt defeated. "You are too cruel. I wish you would consider Fanny's disposition and situation before heaping criticism upon her."

I watched Claire reading, turning thoughts over in my head as she turned her pages. I had no more faith than Shelley in George's acknowledgement of her child as his own, or his taking responsibility for its upbringing. But she *was* my stepsister, and, despite her wayward behaviour, part of the blame for her present condition had to be laid at my door.

She had, by her own admission, always admired my bold pursuit of love and freedom. And my example had shown that love, passion and escape from the apartment above the bookshop were perfectly possible. How could I be surprised if she sought the same for herself?

She had found passion and escape. But unlike me she had not found love. George was flattered by her devotion, but he did not return it. Although her folly exasperated me, I could not bear to contemplate the distress awaiting her. If the fault lay with me, so must the remedy.

"Claire … are you listening?"

She stopped reading and raised her eyes. She looked so beautiful, with the shadow from her straw bonnet brim speckling her rose-petal face, and her lovely bare arms at repose in her lap, that I almost did not have the heart to speak. But I steeled myself.

"Claire, you are going to have a baby, are you not?"

The rose-petal pink changed to a deep red. But, being Claire, she did not flinch. She lowered her eyes and spoke softly. "Yes. You see, my dear sister, a poet is the only kind of lover to have these days."

The memory of this girlish declaration, made in such high expectation of happiness, filled my heart. I leant towards her. "Claire, dear, what does George say he will do?"

Silence. She began to twist her bonnet-strings around her finger. Her eyes moved rapidly beneath her dipped eyelids. She was rehearsing her words, calculating how to exploit my sympathy rather than incur my condemnation.

"He says I am to pretend to be the child's aunt."

"The child's aunt!" I repeated stupidly. "Why?"

"Do you not know that George has a wife living, exactly as Shelley has?" Her large eyes gazed at me soulfully. "He does not think his marriage will survive the scandal."

"And why does he *wish* his marriage to survive? Does he love his wife?"

She twisted the strings more. "Love is only one reason for wishing to retain a marriage."

My expectations of George plunged further. Shelley, impoverished though he was, had been prepared to leave his wife because he loved me. But Claire's words proved that she was aware of George's indifference to her. She had been witness to the fearlessness with which Shelley had faced our outraged parents in the drawing-room, swearing to marry me even though he had not at that time known I had conceived his child. What a contrast she must now see between my lover and hers!

"He will support the child, though?" I asked her. "Even if he will not admit paternity?"

"I do not know what he will do," said Claire, distress creeping into her voice. "At first he said I must keep the child with me, and he will give me money for it. But then he said he will send for the child when it is old enough to go to school, passing it off as his ward, or some such thing."

"What does Shelley say?" I asked, with little hope. "Can he not persuade George to conduct himself like a gentleman in this matter?"

Shrinking under my questions, she began to cry softly. "Nobody can persuade George to do anything," she whispered. "He is his own master."

Her control gone, she put her hands over her face. I left my chair and took her in my arms. She began to sob, her tears soaking my dress. Elise picked up William and advanced across the garden, her face full of concern. I waved her away, instructing her in French to take William off down to the lake.

"George may abandon you," I told Claire, "but Shelley will not. You shall have your confinement in England, and we shall keep the child with us. You may be its aunt in public if George wishes, but in private you may be its mother as much as you like."

She clung to me. She could not speak, but her tears subsided. After I had soothed her for a while, she dried her eyes, trying to smile, and took up her book again.

I walked about the garden until the warmth of the colours and the sunshine had evaporated the agitation in my own heart. In an uncertain world, with an uncertain future, I comforted myself with a pleasing thought. Different though their distresses might be, I could at least do my best by each of my sisters.

Abyss

*F*anny's gold watch was so pretty that Claire implored George to buy her one too. But George's heart had turned to stone; by the time he left for his house in Venice, Claire had neither her watch nor her dignity.

Her sense of self-preservation, however, remained intact.

"I shall be a governess, as you have so often suggested, Mary," she told me as we packed up our belongings at the end of that eventful summer. "I shall support my child myself."

I was unconvinced. "Who would employ a governess who has a child, and is without references?"

"For the price of a gold ring I can pass myself off as a widow," said Claire. "I shall tell them my husband was a soldier and died of cholera in India. My French is fluent, and I know music, and singing, and drawing. Someone in Europe, not England, will take pity on me."

We returned to England with Elise, who had grown very attached to William, as had he to her. She would soon have another charge, of course. Shelley had decided that Elise,

William, Claire and I should be installed in lodgings in the city of Bath, where we would not be recognized and where Claire's baby could be secretly born. Even Mama and Papa were not to be told of the child's existence.

I thought this excessive, and told Shelley so.

"I am acting upon George's instructions," he explained.

I was scornful. "George's instructions! He may have the power to make Claire do whatever he wants, but what power does he have over *you*?"

"He is my friend," he said in a "you would not understand" voice.

I knew he hated my mockery. But *my* spirit was free, even if *his* was enslaved. "Do not allow your admiration for your friend to cloud your judgement of what is clearly right and what is just as clearly wrong," I said.

"Do not lecture me," he replied.

Fanny was delighted with her present, which Claire and I gave her when she had tea with us in our London inn, before we set off for Bath. The colour rose in her pinched face as she drew the watch out of its wrapping.

"Oh, Mary! Claire! How kind you are!" she exclaimed, holding the pretty thing up to the light.

Claire held out her cheek for a kiss, averting her gaze from the expression she knew quite well would be on my face. "How could we forget our dear sister?" she exclaimed.

While we waited for the tea to be brought, Fanny's habitual anxious look returned. She did not pin the watch to her gown, but wrapped it carefully and put it in her bag. I strove to engage her in conversation. "What news of our aunts?" I asked.

Fanny had been living for some months with our mother's two unmarried sisters, an arrangement which had so far proved a welcome relief, for both Fanny and Mama, from the cloud of bitterness which hung over Papa's household.

She bowed her head. "I am to leave their house," she said, "though it causes me much distress."

Claire sat back in her chair, preparing to be bored by the complaints of "Miss Melancholy", as Shelley cruelly nicknamed Fanny.

"My dear Fanny," I said, alarmed, "what has happened?"

"Our aunts have decided to remove to Ireland," said Fanny, her eyes filling with tears.

"Do not you wish to go with them?"

"They do not wish me to join them."

An uneasy silence fell. We all knew that the spinsters' rejection of Fanny could only be explained by her attachment to the scandal caused by Claire and myself.

"Will you go home, then?" I asked. "To Papa's?"

"No!" She wiped her eyes, sniffing. "Do not forget, Mary, Papa is your father but he is not mine. And Claire, Mama is your mother but she is not mine. They have shown me duty, but not love. Without you, Mary, life there is unbearable."

The maid set the tea tray on the table. Fanny tried to compose herself, her thin shoulders rising and falling with the effort. When the servant had gone, Claire leant forward and spoke to Fanny. "Would you like to join our household in Bath, Fanny? It will be cramped, and of course it *is* immoral, but you are very welcome!"

Fanny stared at her coldly. "You never liked me, did you?"

Claire withdrew, and picked up the teapot. "A pretty way to thank me! Do you take milk, Fanny? I do not remember, if I ever knew."

Fanny turned to me. "What can I do, Mary? Where can I go?"

I had no answer. The uncomfortable fact was that although Fanny was frosty, disapproving and difficult to live with, the state in which she now found herself was in part due to the behaviour of Claire and myself. Guilt engulfed me, especially since I alone knew that Fanny was sensible of her faults, kind at heart and desperately in need of love. Most distressing of all, she and our aunts were my only link with my poor dead mama.

"Go home," I advised her. "And I will ask Shelley if there is anything he can do. Perhaps a friend of his knows someone who needs a companion, or a governess…"

Fanny pressed my hand, too overcome to speak.

It was an uncomfortable tea party. When Fanny had gone I voiced my concern about her future, but Claire dismissed it. "Come, Mary, have another cup of tea with me and let us enjoy it. Fanny's face would turn milk sour." She sipped the fresh tea. "*Much* better!"

"But –"

"Mary, enough! Fanny will go home and wait on Mama, and die an old maid like your aunts. Now drink that tea before it is cold."

"Have you no compassion?" I asked, exasperated.

"Yes, I have compassion," she replied. "But I bestow it only where I consider it worthy to do so. I refuse to feel guilty about an evil scandalmonger who deserves to be miserable."

"Oh, Claire!" I was shocked. "How can you say that about Fanny?"

Her cup clattered in its saucer as she leant towards me, her eyes alive with indignation. "You are so simple sometimes! Do you still believe it was *Harriet Shelley* who spread that stupid rumour about Papa selling us for fifteen hundred pounds?"

"Oh, Claire!" I repeated stupidly. My brain did not seem to be working.

"And Fanny has done worse since. She pretends that the gossip starts with Harriet, or Mama, but the real source is Fanny herself, you may be sure. No wonder George does not want her to know about our baby!"

I could not drink my tea. I put the cup down and pushed it away. "Why have you not spoken of this to me before?" I asked.

"Because you seem to care about her, for some unfathomable reason."

I will always regret what I did next. After a sleepless night, I wrote to Fanny, begging her to refute Claire's accusations. By return of post came a letter that chilled my heart. Fanny's indignation spilled from the tearstained pages. The writing was an almost illegible tangle. She accused me of abandoning her to the wolves, of pitching her into the abyss, of destroying her life.

"Wolves? *Wolves?*" said Shelley when I showed him the letter. "What wolves? What abyss? The woman is madder than I thought."

"Shelley, recollect!" I begged. "She has suffered periods of terrible melancholy, almost derangement, in the past. And you of all people, who have known distraction, can you truly ignore her unhappiness?"

I wrung my hands. I paced the room. I could not think what to do.

"Spending a great deal of money on the gift of a gold watch did not work, I see," said Shelley after a pause. "Perhaps sending her to an asylum would be cheaper, and have more effect."

"Shelley!" I cried, aghast. "I expect such words from Claire, but I see you are as heartless as she is!"

This was an accusation I would never, under ordinary circumstances, level at Shelley. His possession of a heart was all too often in evidence. Everything he did was heartfelt, from his belief in freedom for all men to the composition of beautiful verse. I, who shared his nights, knew to what depths this unchecked flow of sensibility could take him. If *he* would not sympathize with Fanny's distress, who in the world would?

The next day we travelled to Bath. A week later, I replied to Fanny's letter. I proposed that I come to London and meet her. Not at my father's house, of course, but at a private room in a hotel. We could dine together, and perhaps I could bring William, whom she had never seen.

But she never read the letter. The next day I received one from her which must have crossed mine in the post. In handwriting even worse than before she told me that she had left home and was going to a place from which she would never return.

"Let us hope she means the Antipodes!" said Claire brightly.

Shelley snatched the letter from my hand. His face had changed as I had read Fanny's words aloud; he knew now that my fears were well founded. "It is marked Bristol," he said.

"For God's sake, Mary, she must be found. I will go at once."

He left the house without bidding us goodbye. Going to the window I saw him give gruff instructions to the man at the hiring stables on the corner. Coins changed hands, then Shelley mounted and galloped towards the Bristol road as if his life depended on it.

I pressed my lips together, fighting tears. He felt guilty at last. He had found his heart again. And my belief in my angel, which had been sorely tried, was restored to me tenfold.

Claire and I waited until the small hours, shivering in our ill-lit parlour after the fire had gone out. I refused to go to bed until I knew Fanny was safe, and Claire relished the drama of the situation. When we at last heard Shelley's boots on the stairs, I stood up, my heart full of dread. But his expression told the news before he spoke.

"You did not find her!" I exclaimed.

"No." He crossed the room and took my face in his hands. His eyes contained the look I had last seen when our baby daughter died. "Dearest…" He released my face and put his arms around me, seeking comfort for himself as much as bestowing it on me. "I fear it is the worst news."

"Do not fear it!" advised Claire, picking up the candle-holder to light herself to bed. "She has probably returned to London by now, having led you all a merry dance."

"No, Claire, she has not." He released me and sank wearily into a chair. "My enquiries led me to an inn where Irish labourers drink. I heard there that a lady answering Fanny's description had been seen boarding a coach for Swansea."

"Swansea?" I had barely heard of this place. "Where is that?"

"It is in the south of Wales. It is the place where ferries depart for Ireland. I thought she might have tried to follow your aunts there, so I hired a carriage to take me to Swansea."

Exhausted, he laid his head against the cushion, closing his eyes.

"What happened?" I whispered, pressing my hand to my rapidly-beating heart.

"I did not have to look for her in Swansea," he said. "Her fate was written on a newspaper vendor's hoarding."

Claire sat down again quickly. She grasped my arm.

Shelley laid the Swansea newspaper on the table for us to read, and went into the bedroom.

Claire and I held the candle over the report. An unknown young woman, it said, had taken a room at an inn and been found dead there, after an overdose of laudanum. She had left a note, but there was no signature.

We clutched each other. "Oh, Mary!" whispered Claire. "It cannot be!"

It was. Fanny had hidden her identity from the Swansea authorities but she could not hide it from us. The young woman's corset, according to the article, was embroidered with "MW". With a rush of grief, I recognized the initials of our mother's unmarried name. But there was further proof. Pinned to the dead woman's gown was a new, exquisitely crafted Swiss gold watch.

When Shelley had gone to identify her body, he told me later, the authorities had offered the watch to him. But, still in debt for it though he was, he had refused.

"I told them to bury it with her," he said. "It was the only beautiful thing she possessed."

Death's Gift

*L*audanum, a common sleeping-draught that Shelley took regularly, is dangerous in large quantities, as Fanny had been aware. Knowing that it contains opium, a narcotic which can cause hallucinations, I had been convinced for some time that it was at the root of the terror that so often gripped Shelley in the middle of the night, and that had so horrified us all as he knelt on the floor at the Villa Diodati. I wished he would not take it at all, however much he longed for peaceful sleep.

But two days after Fanny was buried, I myself resorted to the very substance which killed her. When Shelley and I retired to bed that night, he put some drops of laudanum in warm water and told me to sip it.

I did so. Then I lay down miserably upon my pillow. It was a rainy October night. There was no light from the window, but as my eyes grew used to the darkness I could make out the shape of Shelley's head with its curling hair, and the mound made by his shoulder as he lay on his side. And I could hear his breathing. Fast, steady, attentive.

"Fanny was in love with you," I told him. "Exactly like Claire is still."

He did not speak. My head felt heavy, but my brain raced with thoughts.

"Have you seduced Claire?" I asked.

Still he did not speak.

"Did you tell her it was your birthday?" I taunted. "And did she, poor wretch, believe you?"

"Go to sleep, Mary," he said calmly.

I began to sob with guilt and grief. The bitterness imprisoned in my breast for many months escaped. Jealousy rose again, the same jealousy as I had confronted when Claire had been Jane and had climbed into our bed that night in Switzerland.

I felt his arms around me. He pulled me beside him and did not speak of Claire or Fanny. He soothed me, assuring me of his love. His heartbeat was very fast, but as we lay there, my own heart's frenzy calmed and I began to feel sleepy. The darkness seemed to be falling in on itself.

Shelley pushed the damp strands of hair away from my cheeks. "In the morning you will recollect none of this."

He was wrong, of course. I recollect it now, perfectly well. But I also understand that he said it to spare me remorse. If we could both pretend the words had not been spoken, there would be no need for forgiveness on either side.

Claire was excited at the prospect of motherhood. She fussed over the preparations for the arrival of her baby, directing Elise, who was an excellent needle-woman, in the production of more elaborate baby gowns and bed linen than either of my children had ever owned.

"How clever Elise is!" I exclaimed, fingering the finery which Claire had laid out on her bed for my inspection. "This child will be dressed like a prince!"

"A princess, Mary," said Claire proudly. "I feel sure I will have a girl."

"You were wrong about my first baby."

"Yes, but I was correct about William, if you recall."

I did not recall. "Dear Claire," I said, patting her shoulder.

We were interrupted by Elise, who had been to collect our post. She handed me a letter from Shelley, who was "on business" in London. "On business" was the phrase he used for his fundraising expeditions: a little from his father-in-law here, a little more from a publisher there, loans from three or four friends.

"Thank you, Elise," I said.

I went into the parlour and sat by the fire. It was December, and even with my mittens on, my hands were cold. I warmed them, leaving the letter in my lap. Ever since I had received Fanny's last one I had been wary of opening letters.

Shelley's familiar seal, and my name written in his careless hand, stared at me from the folded paper. I collected my courage and broke the seal.

Can you hear me screaming, Mary? My wife is dead.

My head buzzed. The writing dissolved. I tore at the lace scarf around my neck. I could not breathe. "Claire!" I called.

But my voice was hoarse. She and Elise were chattering, and did not hear me. I closed my eyes, trying to compose myself. When I opened them again my vision had cleared. In disbelief I read on.

Harriet, like Fanny, had killed herself. Her body, apparently several months advanced in pregnancy, had been found in the Serpentine lake in Hyde Park.

Whose child was she carrying? If he has abandoned her, the blame must lie with him, wrote Shelley. Then the letter took on a note of desperation. *I must be allowed to take care of my motherless children now, must I not? Dearest Mary, we shall take Ianthe and Charles away from these shores for ever. Italy will save us. We shall all live in peace there, my children and you and me and William, and Claire and her child, and George.*

George! Grief had unhinged Shelley's mind if he thought George would have anything further to do with us.

I forced myself to read the rest of the letter. Unexpectedly, its desperate tone collapsed at the end into two of the most tender, yet most practical sentences he had ever written to me. *By surrendering herself to death, Harriet has bestowed upon us a gift more precious than any we could give each other. My darling, when will you marry me?*

The events of those few weeks are as difficult to believe as the idea that a scientist could cheat death – and almost as horrific. George's abandonment of Claire, callous though it was, seemed as nothing. The wanton self-destruction of both my sister Fanny and Shelley's wife Harriet was an unimaginable catastrophe. He and I both suffered deeply, plunged into the pitiless darkness that only guilt can cause. Entire, all-consuming, imprisoning.

After Harriet died, Shelley began to take even more laudanum than he had taken before. I would not let myself fear for his life – madness awaited me there – but I cannot pretend I was at ease. All I could hope was that the worst of his suffering would pass quickly, and that he would come back to me, eager for love, life and poetry again.

And as he had foreseen, the dead can affect the living in unforeseen ways.

Two weeks after Harriet's death, he and I entered together the door from which we had been unreservedly banished.

My papa stood by the drawing-room door, rigid with expectation, while Mama gushed a welcome. "My dears!" she exclaimed. "Come in, and sit down by the fire!"

I walked into my father's waiting arms. He held me for a long time, neither moving nor speaking.

"William," said my stepmother's voice, a little shrilly. "Do not neglect your other guest, please."

When I emerged from my father's embrace I was taken, briefly, into hers. Over her shoulder I saw Shelley and Papa shake hands. Then Shelley stood by the fire, courtesy forbidding him to sit down until Mama and I did. He was wearing an expression of deep unease. It was clear we all four were remembering the last occasion we had met in that room, more than two years ago.

"Mama, I have brought you a small gift," I announced, presenting her with one of William's curls encased in a locket.

"My dear Mary, how delightful!" she enthused. I knew she would never wear it, but I had done my duty. "And when are we to meet the little man himself?"

"Whenever you like," answered Shelley. "He is longing to meet his grandpapa, whose name he bears." He glanced at Mama. "And his grandmama, of course."

"Splendid," said Papa with satisfaction. He had recovered

his composure sufficiently to allow conversation. Holding my hand as I sat beside him on the sofa – a place I had never before been allowed to take – he began to ask us about Switzerland, and Lord Byron, and mutual acquaintances. Shelley replied amiably enough, while my attention was monopolized by Mama, who wanted to hear all about William.

Then, during a pause in Mama's questioning, I heard a fragment of the men's conversation. "Excuse me, Mama," I said, and turned to Shelley. "My dear, why are you talking about John Keats?"

Shelley's face relaxed into his warmest smile. "You see, sir," he said to my father, "what a protégé she makes of him?"

"Who?" demanded Mama. "Who is this Keats?"

"He is a young poet," I explained, "quite penniless, dependent upon the goodwill of others for his living. And he is *not* my protégé. If anything he is Shelley's. I merely feel that his talent is worthy, and am interested in his progress."

"If we go abroad again, I will prevail upon him to come and stay with us," said Shelley. "Will that please you?"

"Not if George is there too," I replied, smiling. I addressed my father. "Lord Byron calls him 'Johnny Keats', and says he is an upstart."

Papa understood. "By which he means he is not of the aristocracy, I take it?"

"Exactly," I said. "Such considerations mean nothing to Shelley, of course."

"Of course." Papa looked at Shelley approvingly. "I shall make it my business to procure a copy of Mr Keats's latest poems, and give it to you as a wedding present."

"Thank you, sir," said Shelley, bowing.

When dinner was announced, we sat down in the dining-room of my girlhood as if we had never eaten a meal anywhere else. Tom, who waited upon us, could not forbear to smile at me when he passed with the soup. "Good evening, Miss," he said.

My exile had apparently affected everyone in the house. I was touched, and asked after Tom's wife. Mama, who disapproved of talking to servants during meals except to give orders, tut-tutted, but I took no notice. Her power to command me had diminished now.

When Tom had gone and Mama had made her customary remarks about the temperature of the soup, my father turned a serious eye on me. "We have spoken of Shelley's work, Mary," he said, "and even of that of Mr Keats, of whom I have scarcely heard. But what of your own writing?"

I took two sips of soup during the silence that followed, aware that Shelley was waiting as intently as Papa for my answer. I rarely spoke to Shelley about my growing desire to publish a story. A novel, perhaps, of the kind Claire admired so much. And although he had offered to help me with my writing during my estrangement from my father, I never showed him any of what I considered to be "scribbles" – sketchy, half-planned paragraphs on the backs of the pieces of paper containing his poems, which I gathered up in order to copy neatly for him. The copies made, I never threw the papers away but stored them carefully for my own use.

"I have an idea for a novel," I admitted. "But it is very hazy at present. I cannot even decide upon the end."

"That never stopped a novelist yet, to be sure!" cried Mama. "I cannot count the number of novels I have read with disappointing, muddled endings. I say to William, 'William, you are a writer – why, you should write a book about how to write!'"

While she trilled with laughter at this witty anecdote, I smiled at my father. "I thank you for your enquiry, Papa. I am persevering, and will keep you informed."

Mama had lost the thread of our conversation. When Tom came in to get the soup plates, she signalled him to fill our wine glasses.

"You have talked enough of poetry and novels, my dear," she said to Papa. "This is an occasion to talk of wedding breakfasts and bridal finery, is it not?" She raised her glass. "To marriage!"

We dutifully echoed the toast, and sipped our wine.

"You have been raiding the cellar, sir," said Shelley appreciatively.

My father bowed in acknowledgement. "A fine wine for a happy reunion," he said.

"Indeed," said Shelley, looking at me between the branches of Mama's most elaborate candelabra. "I drink the health of my future wife and her parents with all my heart."

As we drove back to our hotel that evening, I nestled close to Shelley in the carriage. He seemed tired, and did not want to speak.

I could not untangle my feelings. At a stroke, Harriet's despair had made us respectable, bestowed honourable citizenship on our son, and restored my beloved papa to me. I had even been gratified by the greetings of the familiar servants of my childhood. But could happiness and grief sit well together in the same heart? Could Shelley and I truly celebrate, with finery and a wedding breakfast?

I thought not. To the disappointment of Claire and her mama, it was with very little ostentation that I stood beside Shelley a few weeks later in a small London church. Claire wept, Mama smiled, Papa blew his nose and looked at his feet. So, on a damp day in the middle of that winter of damp days, for good or for ill, my romantic poet and I were married at last.

Shelley could not pray. After the
death of Harriet I was forced to the conclusion that an atheist forfeits
the commonplace comfort of prayer when he proclaims his atheism.
Night after night he could not sleep unless he took a draught.
Even when he did, he slept fitfully, often starting up with a cry.
I pitied him from my heart. He was adrift in the isolation
to which he had driven himself.
Under his influence I believed in the power of love and the human
spirit. Together we had discussed the unanswerable questions of
existence, both natural and supernatural. But in moments of agony
I still prayed. When my daughter had died, I had pleaded
with God to give her the eternal bliss that
my dear mama already enjoyed.
But if Shelley could not believe in heaven, in redemption and
forgiveness, what did he suppose had happened to the spirit of this
girl he had loved, who had given him two children and, in despair
beyond any known to him, had drowned herself and her unborn
child? What, in his own moments of agony, did he imagine?
Guilt, a skilful tormentor of even the clearest conscience, plays
havoc with that of an already tormented man. Shelley drank wine,
and brandy when he could get it. When strong liquor failed, he
took opium. That he wept I was certain, though he tried to conceal
this from me. I heard his suffering in the bleakest depths of bleak
nights. I knew his faults, but my love was strong.
"Have no fear, my love," I whispered to him as the first birdsong
began after another empty night. "Fanny and Harriet are at peace,
even if we cannot be."

Italy Will Save Us

$\mathcal{P}$ast scandal, however, is not quickly forgotten.

We were legally married, and William soon had a pretty sister, a baby girl we named Clara, the English version of her aunt's French name. I hoped to live happily with the people I loved, bringing up my children in peace, secure in my father's readmission of me into his society. But Shelley and I were not called upon, nor invited to call. We were unable to penetrate a society in which people desired to protect themselves and their children against irregular households such as ours. The presence of Claire and her child, a little girl named Allegra, whose father was nowhere to be seen, turned suspicious eyes on my new husband. Even the judge in Shelley's petition to gain custody of his eldest children, Ianthe and Charles, ruled that such an immoral man was not fit to be a father.

We decided we must go away again. This time Shelley needed no persuading from Claire and me. He was under the influence of someone else.

"George adores Italy," he informed us one day. "He has

an apartment in Venice, and a summer villa at Padua."

"With mistresses already installed in them?" I asked.

"He believes," Shelley persisted, ignoring my interruption, "that Italy will save us from this infernal gossip we suffer in England. We can settle very contentedly in some pleasant Italian place, where society is more liberal and artistic people gather."

Claire was impressed by this mention of artistic people, a group to which she had always felt she naturally belonged. "Oh, Shelley! If George is not too far away, do you think he will come and visit dear Allegra?"

"There is nothing to stop him," Shelley assured her.

Except his disinclination to do so, I observed to myself.

To Claire's delight, George arranged to join us at our rented villa in Pisa. But when we arrived there, an exhausted party of the three of us, our three children, Elise, and an English nurse with the charming name of Milly, letters awaited us. One, addressed to Shelley, was in George's hand.

"He is not coming," Shelley informed us. "He will send a servant to collect Allegra and take her to stay with him in his house in Venice."

"Why does he want her to go there?" asked Claire, bewildered. "And am I not to go with her?"

"Apparently not," said Shelley abruptly. Then he looked at her, and softened his voice. "Have no fear, my dear Claire. George wants the best for your daughter. Trust him."

I turned away from Claire's stricken face, and Shelley's hollow words, knowing that nothing would lessen the pain of parting with her child. Shelley, of all people, knew this. But he would not side with Claire against George.

In the end, to appease Claire, George allowed Elise to accompany Allegra to Venice rather than sending his own servant. As the carriage carried the screaming child away, and Claire collapsed against me, I felt, though it shames me a little to record this, a measure of relief.

It had been decided that Allegra would remain in her father's charge, leaving Claire free to take the position of governess she had long talked of. All hope of going on the stage had now been discarded. As I comforted her, I wondered whether after all this time Claire might soon cease to be our responsibility?

As the summer wore on, Shelley began to suffer severe pains in his stomach. That he was ill was without question, though he dismissed the seriousness of the symptoms. After three days of vomiting he became feverish. I was alarmed, but no physician we consulted could offer either a diagnosis or a remedy.

"Nervous exhaustion," said one.

"Overwork and anxiety," said another.

"A light diet," said the first.

"Feed him on as much beef and red wine as he can stomach," said the second.

They agreed, however, that an opiate such as laudanum would ease the patient's discomfort. Both recommended larger measures than Shelley had taken before.

He suffered prolonged periods of the derangement we had witnessed at the Villa Diodati. Refusing to go to bed he would wander around the house, or even outside it, in the middle of the night, his eyes glassy and unseeing. He wept and laughed by turns. He could not read, nor write. I prayed to God that our children were too small to remember what they saw.

Claire, immersed in her own sorrow, liked to be near him. She read to him, and made new copies of his poems. She wrote the letters he dictated. I was so busy with housework and children, I knew not what they discussed during the hours they spent together. But gradually she became his confidante. He no longer shared troubles and pleasures with me, but turned instead to her. And slowly, very slowly, he recovered enough of his former strength to take up a pen himself, and set to work again.

In this fashion, strewing the floor around the couch with pieces of paper, written and overwritten with verse, which Claire gathered up and copied, he passed the days. And then, one August afternoon when the shimmering heat of Italy surrounded the villa, pouring in windows and doors and filling up its rooms, we received some news.

Shelley's couch had been placed in the coolest room in the house. He lay there wearing his house robe, and I was sitting at the window sewing, when we heard a shriek from upstairs. Within seconds Claire had pattered down the stairs and entered the room in great agitation. There was a letter in her hand.

"Allegra is ill!" she announced. Her brimming eyes flashed. "She is with Elise at George's villa in Padua!"

"And where is George?" I asked.

She consulted the letter. "Still in Venice. He cannot get away."

"Why not?"

Ignoring me, she folded the letter and gazed tearfully at Shelley. "I must go to my daughter!"

"Indeed you must," said Shelley calmly. "I shall take you there."

I was astonished. "But George, even if he is in Venice, will not allow it!"

"George will not know," Shelley declared. "But if he finds out, I wager that he will do what is right when a child's life is in danger."

"And what about *your* life?" I protested. "You are not well enough to travel to Padua!" I turned to Claire, who stood with the letter in her hand, her face flushed, her tears drying. "*You* do not think Shelley is well enough to come with you, do you? You must go alone!"

Shelley spoke before Claire could open her mouth. "A lady cannot travel alone in Italy, as you well know, Mary. And we have no male servant." He rose from the couch. "Make haste," he instructed Claire. "We must leave immediately."

"I am to stay here with Milly and the children, I suppose?" I asked.

"Of course," said Shelley, half rising from the sofa, his arm half out of the sleeve of his robe. "For pity's sake, the children cannot travel such a distance in this heat!"

If only I had had the courage to hold him to those words. They haunt me to this day, though Shelley never afterwards admitted uttering them.

"Oh, Shelley!" cried Claire, falling on her knees at his feet. "How good you are!"

I regarded my husband coldly. "Do what you will," I told him, "but be sure that George will discover what you have done."

He glared at me. "What if he does? He will hardly throw the mother of his child into the streets."

"That is what you believe, is it?"

"Silence!" he commanded.

Then he closed his eyes, and put his hands to his temples. "My head aches," he sighed. "Mary, I do not want to lose George's friendship over this. He will not see Claire. But at least she may see her child, who needs her. Leave it to me."

Standing up, he helped Claire to her feet. "All will be well," he assured her. Then he took my hand, and kissed my cheek. "You are a good girl, my dear. But you must trust that *I* am good, too. I will return almost before you have noticed I am gone."

I *did* notice he was gone, however. And during the long, light August evenings, as I sat alone, writing, when the children were asleep, I thought about him and Claire in the empty villa, and wondered what right he had to demand my trust when he had so seldom proved worthy of it.

Into the Depths

*I*taly baked under a heatwave. Continuous sunshine had dried up streams and stunted crops. Animals lay dead in the fields. Pisa itself shimmered as if enveloped in a brilliant veil worn by an Indian bride. In such heat, we might as well have been in India.

One night, about a week after Shelley and Claire had departed, baby Clara refused to sleep. Nothing we did could soothe her. Milly, who adored all the children and had wept when Elise had been compelled to take Allegra away, could not conceal her anxiety.

"Clara has a fever," she informed me. "What shall I do?"

I instructed her with more calm than I felt. "Fetch me a cloth and some water, and go to bed. I will watch by Clara tonight, and bathe her. If she is no better in the morning we must call a physician."

Memories crowded my brain. My other daughter, lying in her cradle with her cheek on her fist. Cold, cold, cold. On that English February night I had had no warning of the battle with death my firstborn was to have, but this time, in the relentless Italian heat, I was prepared. Small – less than a year old – and weak my dear Clara might be, but if death threw down the gauntlet, I would fight it with my own life.

That wakeful night passed slowly, but in the morning Clara was cooler. I decided there would be no need for a physician. Milly went as usual to collect our post, and when she returned she held out to me a letter addressed in Shelley's handwriting.

Letters. Always letters. In my dreams and out of them.

George had invited us *all* to the villa in Padua, Shelley informed me. The letter described the beauty of the villa, the sweetness of the air, the perfection of the situation and aspect. I was to bring Milly and the children as soon as possible.

I did not understand. What could be Shelley's motive for wanting us to go to Padua, when only a week ago he had been so adamant that we stay in Pisa?

I went straight to my writing-desk and informed him of Clara's illness. As he had himself observed, children – especially a sick baby – could not travel in such heat.

But indignation was stamped plainly on his reply. *Mary, why can you not accept the simplest request?* it demanded. *I want my family with me, and I want to accept my friend's invitation. Is that unreasonable? Why are you continually placing obstacles in my way? Clara is past the dangerous age, and a robust child. Kiss her and William for me, cease complaining and come as soon as you can.*

Girlish rebelliousness, such as Claire had so admired, rose in my breast when I read these words. But I had to quash it. I was not a girl any more. I was the mother of two children, and we all depended upon my husband for money and protection.

I did not wait for the threats I knew would follow another refusal. I scribbled a hasty note, agreeing without enthusiasm to go. Then Milly, the children and I set off on the long, dry road to Padua.

Clara, still feverish and with a livid rash on her body, was as weak as the day she was born. She seemed to be waiting for the end of the nightmare with fortitude. She did not cry, nor demand to be cradled. She could neither suck nor swallow. As I watched her I felt the same stone-dead weight in my stomach as had been there when Fanny died. *This is my fault, this is my fault, this is my fault.* My daughter was dying because I had not protected her. Because I, too, was weak.

When we arrived at the villa I could not bring myself to greet Shelley warmly. His concern at Clara's condition was eclipsed by the contentment that neither he nor Claire could disguise. Shelley's appearance bore witness to a more rapid rate of recovery than he had achieved in Pisa, and Claire's blood, as ever, pinkened her cheeks.

"Where are Allegra and Elise?" I asked.

"Allegra has recovered, and they are gone back to Venice," explained Claire.

Taking the baby into a bedchamber, I cradled her in my arms and wept, longer and more bitterly than I had ever wept. Allegra had never been ill at all. There had been no letter from Elise. Shelley and Claire had concocted the story in order to be alone together in George's villa.

That he had now seduced her was clear. They had been in Padua for almost a month. Claire's radiant appearance was not due to Allegra's deliverance, though of course she would insist it was. And I knew her well enough to see the futility of writing to Elise to demand her contradiction of their story. Claire was too clever not to have silenced the nurse-maid by some means.

"Is George expected to join us here?" I asked Shelley that evening, as I sat with Clara on my lap in George's comfortable drawing-room. Shelley was lying on the sofa, and Claire played untidy fragments on the piano.

I watched Shelley's face. He tried not to allow his expression to change. "You know he cannot come, my dear."

"And yet he insists on allowing us the use of his servants, his larder and his cellar! His kindness is truly extraordinary!"

"Quite so," said Shelley.

There was awkwardness in his voice. He was betrayed. I seized upon it.

"George extended his invitation several weeks ago, when you were ill, did he not?" I asked. Claire stopped playing. Shelley sat up.

"But unbeknown to George," I went on, "you and Claire decided to come here alone." I kept my voice low, for Clara's sake. "You only sent for your wife and children when you could no longer pretend that we had been 'delayed', or whatever excuse you gave him. He thinks we have *all* been here the whole time, does he not?"

"My dear, you mistake everything," he protested.

"I mistake nothing. You subjected our baby to a journey she was too ill to make, in order to conceal from George that you were living alone with the woman *he too* has seduced and discarded. I shall never again believe anything you say."

Claire had the good sense to remain silent. But Shelley, incapable of admitting defeat, tried to defend himself.

"What proof do you have of this, Mary? Have you —"

He stopped, his face freezing. Clara had begun to convulse so violently that she almost fell to the floor. Her rigid little body jerked uncontrollably. It was so pitiful, Claire ran out of the room with her hands over her face.

Shelley collected his wits. "Get your cloak," he commanded me. "We must take her to Venice, to George's English doctor. He will save her."

We took her to Venice, but the doctor never saw her. As I waited alone in a hotel for Shelley to bring him, Clara had one last seizure and died in my arms.

The Act of Creation

Rome, 8 June

My dearest Papa,

Of all the letters I have written or received in my life, this one bears the hardest news.

Our darling William, your namesake, your only grandson and our last remaining child, last evening surrendered to death. Weep, Papa, and be assured I weep too, whatever hour of the day or night this reaches you!

After the terrible events of last summer I thought that I had reached the bottom of a pit of darkness. But I had further to fall. My only boy has died from malaria, a disease unknown in England, which kills swiftly and for which there is no cure. Lord Byron once told Shelley *that Italy would save us. But instead it has killed both our children,*

and will, I fear, be our final resting place too.

William is to be buried in the Protestant cemetery here in Rome.

As soon as we can, we are going to remove ourselves to another part of

Italy ~ I know not where. But I am determined that my next child,

which I expect in November, shall be born away from the pestilence

that killed my precious boy. If only I could come home to England!

Papa, I am more wretched than I know how to express. I shall send

our new address as soon as I am able. Until then, God be with you, as

he is evidently not with me.

I signed my name and blotted the ink. I folded the letter and sealed it, and wrote my father's address and blotted it again. I left it on the table in the hall of our lofty Roman apartment, for Milly to post. Then I went into the drawing-room and opened the glass doors to the balcony.

I was alone. Earlier that afternoon, Shelley, Claire, Milly and I had set off for the Protestant chapel where William's body had been taken. But my nerve had broken before we left the apartment building. As I sank to the floor in the lobby, Shelley had stopped my fall and carried me to a chair, where Claire had fanned me while Milly, grave-faced, waited in the doorway. When I had recovered a little, Shelley and Claire had decided that I was unequal to the task of saying farewell to my son, and should stay at home, writing the letters necessary after a death.

"You may still attend the chapel in the morning, Mary," Claire had told me, folding up her fan, "and pray for William then."

The street looked a very long way below. The carriages, the narrow bodies of horses and the stumpy, foreshortened passers-by looked like toys. It was early evening. The shadows were lengthening, though the air was still very warm. I was clad in black, with a veil around my shoulders with which to cover my head in the street. I had bought these clothes last year, for Clara's funeral.

Looking down was making me dizzy. Instead I gripped the rail and looked up. The Italian sky reached upwards for ever, with the astonishing clarity of light only Mediterranean skies possess. The coming of evening had done little to dim it.

I thought of that night in Switzerland, at the Villa Diodati, when the sight of the sunset and the storm clouds over the lake had so troubled me and yet inspired me with the fervour of the storyteller.

"I know you have a story to tell," George had said that night, "and one day, like the ancient mariner, you will be compelled to tell it."

I went in and wandered restlessly around the room. Some fire was in me. Some desire for I knew not what.

Shelley had left a pile of books on the table. They were all well-known to me – I had packed and unpacked them a hundred times. Among them I spied the green cover of his collection of poems by Coleridge. That same Mr Coleridge who had sat in my father's drawing-room and recited *The Rime of the Ancient Mariner*, the tale of a man condemned by a curse to tell his tragic story to any listener. Claire had slept on the sofa while I had listened, entranced.

I opened the book and read the first lines of the poem. My heart leapt at the sight of the familiar words. Already fraught with memories, they were invested now with a new power of the story over the storyteller.

I put the book down. Standing there in that lonely room I was aware of the presence of something powerful. Present and past grief, fear for the future, love, jealousy and the desire to mend my spirit swirled together like a torrent. I yearned for peace, for escape. But like the cursed ancient mariner, as George had foretold, I would never be free until I had rid my soul of the tale it had nurtured for so long.

Deep inside me another life stirred. My new baby was making its first fluttering movements. I pressed my hand to my belly, overcome with love as I had been at this moment with all my other children. But this time, fearful for the child's future as I had never been before.

The creation of life is a wonderful and unfathomable thing, to be sure. But death is swift. In my first baby's case, too swift even for her to be given a name. For Clara, before she had even learnt to walk. And for my dear William, who only a month ago had sat for his portrait with the merriest smile you ever saw...

These thoughts brought tears, but I controlled them. The fire in my heart had not abated. Indeed, memories were fanning its flames. George was right. The time had come for me to spill my soul before the world, and tell my story of the act of creation of the living from the dead. How could I fail to be fascinated with the idea that some day, death could be conquered, and that the anguish our mortality imposes upon those who survive us will be banished for ever?

The deepening blue of the sky beckoned me out to the balcony again. I gazed up in despair and wonder. And as I did so, the ending of the tale came to me.

My mother. My firstborn. Fanny. Harriet. Clara. William. All these lives had ended, innocent though they were. And if innocents die, I reasoned, how could I let a guilty man live? I had long pondered on this, but now I made my decision. My scientist, whose desire to play God led him to create a monster, must indeed be punished for his arrogance by death. I would send him to the place where so many people I loved had gone. Like them, he would die in misery. Not from disease or by his own hand, but because my conscience could not let him live.

Creatures *did* kill their creators. I had dreamt that I had murdered my own mother. If a woman could be destroyed by a child, why could not a man create a being that ultimately destroyed *him*?

My heart bursting, I returned to the drawing-room. I sat down once more at the writing-desk and drew a piece of paper towards me. Then, in a fever, I seized a pen and began to write.

Resurfacing

*G*rief, and the betrayal I could not forgive, made me lash out at the person I should have cherished. "*You* are the instrument of our poor children's deaths!" I declared.

My power to cause Shelley pain was great. And, suffering as I was from my own pain, I did not shrink from using that power. "If you were strong, a man who knows what is right and what is wrong, they would be living still!"

His face was like a mask. Bloodless, stiff, without expression. But I was unmoved. This time he could not calm me with laudanum.

"If only *you* had not made me bring Clara to Padua, to cover your deception of George, she would yet be alive! If only *you* had not insisted we come to Rome, where the disease which killed William flourishes, he would yet be alive!"

Shelley did not move, but his cheeks suddenly reddened and his eyes shone with tears. I saw this, but I did not stop.

"Two children from the same family do not die within a year of each other unless there is adult selfishness, or neglect, or corruption," I told him. "Ianthe and Charles, Harriet's children, remain with their grandparents, perfectly well. But *my* children are dead because *you* have murdered them!"

He leapt out of his chair and, reaching into the pocket of his breeches, produced his penknife.

"Kill me, then, Mary!" he demanded. In his face there was a madness which, in all his moments of madness, I had never beheld. "Kill me now! If your hatred and your will are strong enough, take this knife and kill me!"

I sat down trembling. "My will *is* strong," I told him. "But having been the cause of my mother's death I have no desire to be the cause of anyone else's."

"Yet you *will* kill me, with or without this knife," he said testily, putting it back in his pocket. "You will starve me of your love, until I die."

Before me stood the man for whom I had abandoned my girlhood, my family and my reputation. But the task of rebuilding our happiness seemed as daunting as scaling the icy wall of a mountain.

And it was as an icy wall that Shelley appeared. He and I could not share our grief; he had withdrawn his love because he considered my response to our children's deaths cold. But my coldness was born of despair. No one would comfort me – not even my father, who begged me repeatedly to leave Shelley and come back to England, and certainly not Claire, whose only child yet lived.

She did not know this loss, greater than any other. Only Shelley knew it, but he refused to mourn with me. He folded up his feelings as he might a poem scrawled on a piece of paper, and hid them away. Neither I nor anyone else could touch them. So we suffered alone, apart and in silence.

Meanwhile, reckless, idle, deceitful Claire at last secured a post as a governess.

"A delightful family," she announced. "Two adorable little girls, and a house full of servants, overlooking the bay at Livorno."

"Delightful," I echoed.

I was relieved that she was leaving, though I might have wished her farther away from Pisa, where we had now returned, than Livorno. For years I had had good reason to despise her, though I had tolerated her presence for the sake of the affection we had known in girlhood. But her part in poor Clara's death had torn a hole in our sisterly companionship larger than either of us could mend.

"Will you escort me there, Shelley?" she asked sweetly. "Please?"

"Of course," he agreed. "But I must come straight back. Mary's confinement is near."

I watched them exchange the kind of glance I had seen so often. How I longed to tell Claire the truth: that if Shelley had made love to her under our own roof, even in our own bed, I would have tolerated this in exchange for my daughter's life. But the way she had conspired with him to save her own face, despite the danger to her little namesake Clara, had hardened my heart against her for ever.

"Must you go at all, my dear Claire?" Shelley asked. "After all, with the new baby…"

"Yes, she must," I declared.

Since William's death my tolerance of Shelley's desire for both my sister and myself, his beloved two-headed goddess, had evaporated. Fearing the fury in my voice, he gave in.

"Yes, I suppose she must. It is for the best."

After Claire's departure, the distance between Shelley and me widened even further. I could not forgive him for his betrayal and the suspicions that tormented me still. Had he promised to continue his affair with Claire in return for her taking the governess post? Did he burn her correspondence? How often would he insist on going to Livorno?

Shelley was even less forgiving than I. He did not forgive me for accusing him of our children's murder. He did not forgive me for insisting that we rid ourselves of Claire. And he did not forgive me for being the person he loved better than Harriet.

"Why did you agree to elope with me?" he asked one evening, gazing at my misshapen body as I lay on the sofa, trying in vain to sleep. "Why did you not send me back to Harriet?"

No answer was possible. I was silent.

"If you had not been so attractive, and willing, Harriet would never have drowned herself. And even if she had, it is your insistence upon staying with me that has made the judge refuse me custody of Ianthe and Charles," he said.

I could not allow him to heap on my head the guilt that should have been on his. I had to speak.

"I suppose you have conveniently forgotten the presence of another man's child inside Harriet's corpse?" I demanded. "Why is it *my* morals, not hers – or indeed yours – which are now called to account?"

"You are cruel," he complained. "You will kill me yet."

"And I am supposed to feel sorry for you?"

When Shelley slept, or was out of the house, I wept. Secretly, I prayed. I placed my faith in the knowledge that the light of the sun in the east, which begins as a pinpoint on the horizon and grows into a brilliant arc before the eyes of the transfixed observer, conquers darkness not once, but daily, for eternity.

And light *did* come back, as gradually as that eternal dawning. My second son was born.

William had borne my father's name; our new son bore my husband's. Shelley's first name was Percy, a kingly name from the pages of English history, which his family had bestowed on its members for generations. He had always disliked it and never used it, but he granted my wish.

"I care not what his name is," he said, stroking the baby's face. "I only care that he lives to pass it on to his own children."

"God grant that," I murmured.

"It is not the will of God that determines such things," he said.

As has often been observed, the toiling creative mind is driven hardest when suffering is at its height. During those terrible months, both Shelley and I retreated from the world, depending on our writing to calm us. My manuscript was contained in a leather letter-case – a gift from Papa long ago – which I could close up and pretend held only letters if anyone should approach. Shelley knew that I was writing a story, and he said he would be interested to read the result. But he no longer attempted to give me advice on its writing; he knew how jealously I guarded it.

Poems, and fragments of poems, lay around the house on torn pieces of paper, or untidy notebooks, or were scribbled on the back of letters, or lists, or on the flyleaves of books. I collected them together, taking over Claire's former employment of making fair copies and insisting that Shelley prepare the manuscripts for publication. I would not allow his casual approach to the business of publishing bar his path to poetic immortality. It lay within his grasp, as George and I well knew. As for my leather-bound manuscript, in its hiding-place under my gowns in a trunk … its future was less certain.

The first year of Percy's life wore on. He was a winter baby, though this caused me little anxiety, as the months of cold, damp weather that endanger babies in England are not among Italy's hazards. Winter brought falling leaves, and cool breezes. The sun on the hillsides made long, blue shadows. And my son celebrated his first birthday in good health.

Gradually, Shelley's mood changed. The first thing I had ever admired him for – his reckless disregard for any attempt to stop him doing what he wanted – returned. He became restless.

"Mary, I am determined to get George down to the coast with us next summer," he declared. "I am wild to sail again, as we did in Geneva."

I looked up from my reading. "Is George an experienced enough sailor? There is a great difference between Lake Geneva and the open sea."

"Of course he is!" Then, after some thought, "Or he has an experienced boy, at least."

I smiled. "And does he have a boat?"

"He is having one built as we speak," he said eagerly, crouching beside my chair with some of the boyish enthusiasm I had thought I would never see again. "A splendid vessel, to be called the *Bolivar*."

I touched his cheek. Fleetingly, some of our past intimacy returned. Shelley seized my hand.

"Mary, I can bear this living death no longer. You and I must live again. We were drowning, but we will resurface."

Sailor

When I suggested that Shelley seek the company of our new neighbours, I thought that entering the lives of strangers would distract him from his reckless desire to be a sailor. But I could not have been more mistaken.

"An English couple have taken that white villa you always say looks like a wedding cake, not half a mile from here," I announced one spring day, without looking up from my writing. "Milly has met their maidservant, who told her they have a little boy and another child expected. They are called Williams. You might introduce yourself to them, if you have nothing better to do."

Shelley approved. "Why, let us call on them tomorrow!"

But there was no need. They called on us, greeting us warmly as soon as Milly showed them into the hall.

"What a happy circumstance," said Jane Williams, smiling brilliantly as she entered the salon, "that your son is so near ours in age!"

"Indeed," agreed Shelley. He turned to her husband. "Shall we walk in the garden, while the ladies converse? I prefer air and exercise over salon talk, and perhaps you do too."

Edward Williams bowed, and allowed himself to be led outside. I knew what Shelley was doing. He wanted to find out the couple's background before we disclosed ours, and he was well aware that women alone can achieve this far quicker than in mixed company.

"I understand your husband is a poet," began Jane Williams when they had gone. "His fame goes before him in Pisa, I must tell you!"

"He is indeed," I told her proudly. "And what is your husband's profession?"

To my surprise, she blushed, and hid her face behind her fan. "Edward is not my husband," she admitted. "The gossip that pursues us in England has driven us to settle here, in good time for the birth of our new baby."

So she knew my background already, then. If she had not, she would not have disclosed such intimate facts about her own at our first meeting. She and Edward knew that we, too, had run away from scandal.

My heart warmed towards her. "Has Edward a wife living?" I asked.

"No." She closed the fan. Her composure was returning, but the lids of her large eyes remained lowered. "But I am not free. I married in haste at sixteen. My husband was … unsatisfactory, so when I met Edward…"

"I understand," I said, with feeling.

"He was as you see him now: handsome, full of life. I ran away with him. I took his name and live with him as his wife. I will never go back."

I extended my hand. "Jane… May I call you Jane?"

She nodded, extending her own hand. I noticed how small

it was, smaller even than Claire's. Our fingertips touched.

"The similarities in our circumstances are striking," I observed. "I wonder whether Shelley has found things in common with Mr Williams?"

"Oh! Call him Edward, please. And I doubt it," she added, giggling. "Edward is a seafarer."

My heart quickened. "Is that so?"

"He was a captain in the navy, although, disappointingly, he never served under Admiral Nelson himself. His passion is the sea." Her smile widened. "I cannot imagine a poet and a sailor will find much to speak of."

"Do not believe it!" I told her. "Shelley shares the same passion. He will be overjoyed to meet someone who actually knows how to sail."

"Oh, Edward does not know how to sail!" exclaimed Jane. "He leaves it to his boy!"

As the spring wore on, Edward and Jane Williams became our constant companions. I respected Jane for her calm beauty, and her intelligence. And her story had touched my heart; she, like me, had been cast adrift as a result of falling in love. Attending at her confinement, I admired her baby girl and enjoyed the company of these new friends.

I knew I had to lift up my head and live again. I had not yet celebrated my twenty-third birthday, and Italy was not the place for sadness or jealousy.

It remained, however, the place for death.

"Alas!" cried Shelley one morning, his eyes scanning a letter that arrived from a literary friend in London. "Mary, we shall never have the pleasure of John Keats's company after all. He is dead!"

I put down my own letter, from Claire. Though Shelley's acquaintance with Keats was small, and my own had been conducted entirely through the young man's poetry, I could not but be moved. "How?" I asked bleakly.

"'Of consumption,'" read Shelley, "'in Rome.' He is buried in the same cemetery as our dear William."

"Oh!" My heart convulsed in my breast and I put my hand to my throat. "Poor Keats! What a tragedy, to die so young and in possession of such genius!"

Shelley looked up, his eyes alight. "Indeed, Mary, it *is* a tragedy. I must write to George."

He sat down at the writing-desk and chose a pen. "Where have you put that volume of Keats's poems your father gave us?" he asked. "I must reread his lines."

Claire's letter contained more pleasing news. It seemed that my husband's scheming concubine had been removed even farther away from us. The Livorno family had not lasted long as Claire's employers, and she was now living in Florence. In the last words of the letter she even hinted she may take a position in *Russia*, a notion I could not but applaud.

"How is Claire?" asked Shelley, scribbling busily.

"The same."

I did not choose to speak of Claire to Shelley. I knew he received letters from her and burned them.

But as the year wore on, the increasing warmth of the sun melted grief and suspicion. I began to believe, as Shelley had promised, that we would surface, and live again.

It gave me joy to see Shelley and Edward shed the formality of early acquaintance and form a friendship fuelled by their love of sailing. They hired a small boat, which they took out every day on the canal that runs between Pisa and Livorno.

Shelley learned quickly. He was soon boasting that he knew the handling of boats better than George, and was looking forward to mocking his wealthy friend's ham-fistedness.

"George's boat is almost completed," Shelley announced one evening when the Williamses were dining with us. "He is impatient to sail it."

He glanced at Edward, who took up his part readily. "Shelley and I have a plan."

"Oh, a plan!" exclaimed Jane, looking at Edward with her languorous eyes. "Why do men always have to have a *plan*?"

"Do not jest, my dear, we are in earnest," said Edward. "What do you ladies say to moving to the coast? We shall take one villa only, to save money, and Shelley can have his own boat built."

"Why?" Jane and I asked together.

The next question was obvious to both of us, but it was Jane who voiced it. "Edward, dear, is not the sea around this coast dangerous?"

Edward kissed Jane's hand. "I am honoured by your concern," he told her. "But remember, my love, I have survived the tempests of the Cape on several occasions."

I was not convinced. "I agree with Jane," I said to Shelley. "The plan to live together is a good one, but I must question the wisdom of buying a boat. Where will the money come from?"

"Mary, do not trouble yourself over such things," he said. "Do you think I plan to have a craft the size of George's *Bolivar*? Of course not!"

"There, Jane, you see?" said Edward, smiling affectionately at her. "Even Mary's common sense will not deter Shelley from sailing on the sea. His appetite for adventure will never be satisfied."

"Shelley cannot swim, Edward," I ventured.

"No more can I," said Edward.

They both burst into laughter, and I knew my case was lost. But after dinner, when Jane and I had retired to the salon, our conversation returned to the subject.

"They are all for going to the coast, Mary, and getting Lord Byron to join them there," she said anxiously. "Tell me, is Lord Byron a knowledgeable sailor? And is he less reckless than Edward and Shelley?"

I could not help but laugh outright. Unsettled, Jane waited with a frown. "Why do my words amuse you?" she asked solemnly.

"Oh, Jane! I am not laughing at your words," I assured her, "I understand your fears only too well. But if I could only begin to describe the way Lord Byron approaches life!"

"Why? Is he as wild as he is reported to be?"

I composed myself, and considered. "Perhaps ... it is best to say that his desires sometimes exceed his prudence, and he is wealthy enough to indulge them."

"Alas!" cried Jane, and put her hand over her mouth.

"Do not make yourself unduly anxious," I added, more optimistically than I felt. "George has none of Shelley's childish abandon. He is a calculating man, who would not risk his life merely for the sake of adventure."

Her eyes looked into mine, over the hand she still held to her mouth. Then she took her hand away, and grasped my own hand with it. It felt damp from her breath. "But Edward would," she said softly. "There is a madness in him. And that madness, I feel sure, has touched Shelley."

I thought I was dreaming.

I thought I was being carried across a calm ocean in a boat, rocking like a baby in its mother's arms, content. But as I surfaced from sleep I realized I was truly being rocked, by Shelley repeatedly rolling against me. I sat up and, fumbling in the dark for a tinderbox, lit the candle in the stand on my side of the bed. I held it aloft and looked at Shelley in the small light it shed.

He was sweating, and the skin on his face had the cold, white sheen of fear it took on when his mind detached itself from reality and he sank into nightmare.

"Shelley!" I whispered, trying to restrain him with my free arm. I was too weak – he continued to roll like a lunatic in a straitjacket. "Shelley, wake up!"

His eyes were staring but he did not seem to be awake. I was afraid. Putting down the candle I tried with both arms to calm him, but he was stronger when demented than when rational. "Allegra!" he shouted. "Allegra, I am dying!"

Oh, God. It was two weeks now since we had received the news that Claire's child had died of typhoid at the convent school where George had insisted upon sending her. A distraught Claire had visited us at Pisa, throwing herself upon Shelley as if she had decided to employ him, and only him, as her comforter. Day and night he had borne her grief-induced hysteria. She had fought him and he had restrained her. She had screamed like an animal, keeping Percy awake, and Shelley had talked to her for hours, until she was calm again. The strain of this unlooked-for appointment, and the resulting lack of sleep, had pushed him further into dependence upon opium.

"How much have you taken?" I demanded. Reaching across him,

my heart filling with panic, I felt for the bottle beside the bed. In the candlelight I saw it was almost empty.

"My Allegra, my darling…" he murmured. "Claire, dearest…"

He sat up suddenly, his hands clutching his head. "See my blood? I am covered in blood!" he groaned, lying down again and squirming in evident, though imagined, agony.

As I was powerless to end the nightmare, I did what I had become accustomed to do. I lay as far away from him as I could, on the very edge of the bed, all my senses alert, facing him so that he could not attack me unawares.

By the morning he would have sunk into torpor, his face as white as the pillow he lay on, the veins in his eyelids showing blue.

When he awoke, about midday, he would have no recollection of the apparitions that had peopled the darkness and made him scream.

And I had learned, after so many years, to make no mention of it.

Don Juan

The villa we moved into with the Williams family was on the coast near the village of Lerici, in the north-west of Italy. The location was wild, the house primitive and the dialect of the local people incomprehensible. We felt as if we had taken a step into an alien world.

That Lerici was a beautiful place was not in doubt, but housekeeping and care of the children was not easy in such an inaccessible place. A few days after our arrival I remarked to Shelley that we might as well be on a South Sea island for all our contact with society.

He beamed at me, squinting against the sun, which streamed into the garden where we were trying to dig a vegetable patch. "My dear Mary, what more could you desire? There is clean water, and a fire, and beds in the bedrooms."

I sighed, straightening my aching back. "I suppose so. But there are not going to be any vegetables until rain has softened this earth, and it will be months before that happens."

"Let us stop this pitiless task, then," he suggested, "and be thankful."

I did my best to get used to life at Lerici, but something prevented my nerves from settling. I had difficulty sleeping, and suffered sudden rapid beatings of my heart.

I did not forget the fear I had felt during Shelley's latest nightmare, but I stored the memory of it in a deep, seldom-visited place. Allegra joined the ghosts of children I had loved, whose spirits slumbered by day and hovered on the edge of my repose by night.

And Claire … Claire no longer had any power to pain me. Her own pain had raised her higher in my affections than she had been for years. What did love for a man signify when it is love for a child that holds the real power over women? Claire had learned that brutal lesson in the most brutal way.

I was again expecting a child. Every day I prayed that God would send me a daughter, and not take her away again as He had her sisters.

"Do not be morbid," chided Shelley. "You are always the same in the early months. Believe in life, not God. Do not pray, but love, and all will be well."

The summer gathered momentum. By early June, hot day followed hot day with a relentless certainty which, however long I lived in Italy, astonished my English sensibility. No clouds, no wind, not a drop of rain or dew. I took to rising early, as the heat of the day burst over the horizon, before the sun was high enough to drive us indoors.

One glorious morning I pulled a light shawl over my nightdress and went down to the beach. I stood at the water's edge, thinking about the past. The sea melted tantalizingly into the distance, full of the same promises of love and adventure that had brought me to Europe all those years ago, when I had been a girl of sixteen in body but a woman in spirit.

I seated myself on a rock, and pondered. My body was a woman's now: I had borne four children, and was soon to bear another. The muscles in my back and legs had become strong from strenuous walking among mountains and the rocks of this unforgiving coastline. Yet I felt drained, as if my blood were too thin. Adjusting my shawl, I examined my veins. They threaded their bluish-green way from my wrists to my forearms, then disappeared deep into my flesh like underground rivers.

This flesh had endured much, and the spirit it enclosed had been driven to the brink of disintegration. Where was that unshackled dreamer who had soaked her dress and flirted with Shelley in the shop that day? Where was the witchery he had fallen in love with? A wild spirit, my father had called me. Had loss and estrangement suffocated that spirit, or was it awaiting the right moment, when circumstances demanded, to burst forth again?

Something was flickering on the horizon. I stood up, waiting and watching. What I had seen was the sparkle of the sun's rays glancing off the mast of a sailing boat. I stretched my neck. Yes, it was the right boat. Yes, it was approaching the shore. And yes, the right man stood like a figurehead on the deck, shouting greetings and waving what looked like a torn petticoat.

I waved back. The boat, which I knew was the *Don Juan* even before the lettering on its hull came into view, glided peacefully nearer and nearer the beach. Hanging on the ropes was a young boy with a scarf tied about his neck. He was laughing. He looked picturesque, I thought, with his bare toes curled around the ropes like a cat's paws.

"Where is Shelley?" called George from the deck.

"Asleep!"

"On a perfect day like this?" He dropped his white ensign – I was right, it was a petticoat – and leapt into the shallow water.

I hurried between the rocks, the sun hot on my bare head. "Why are you so late, George?" I scolded. "Poor Edward and Shelley have watched for you these four days."

He reached the tide line and stood before me on the pebbly sand, his eyes appraising my appearance from between strands of wet, sand-blotched hair. However many times I saw George, I could never resist the notion that he was more of the air than the earth. Or perhaps, indeed, a creature of the sea.

"What matter? I am here now." He took my hand and kissed it. "All I require is my fellow sailors, if their beautiful wives can spare them, and we can be off."

I did not protest. George's influence over Shelley was at the bottom of this scheme: flushed with the idea of being master of his own boat, George had encouraged Shelley in a similar plan. "You cannot dwell on this delightfully wild coast and not have a boat!" he had declared. Shelley, of course, needed no further entreaty.

Edward's friend Trelawny and another ex-naval officer, Captain Roberts, had designed and built George's boat, the *Bolivar*. Shelley, too, had ordered a boat from Trelawny and Roberts, and it was this vessel, the *Don Juan*, that George and the boy had now sailed down the coast from the boatyard at Livorno to her new master.

Shelley, Edward and George were planning to set off on

what they called a sea voyage, though Jane and I foresaw that the "voyage" would only be around the headland and back, in the sunshine, accompanied by much wine and singing.

The boy had moored the boat and was sitting in the bow, dangling his legs over the side, awaiting his captain's orders. I seized the moment.

"George, will you look after Shelley?"

His eyes narrowed. "My dear child, if you are so anxious, why not prevail upon Shelley to abandon the whole enterprise?"

"How can I? You know that the boat is a toy he must play with until he is bored with it."

Ever since that frightful night at the Villa Diodati, George had respected my intelligence, and sharpened his own wit upon it. He listened to me.

"George, it is a fault in Shelley's character that he takes everyone to be exactly as they present themselves," I said.

He nodded. "And when his idols are discovered to have feet of clay, naturally he will never admit to his former idolatry."

"Exactly."

"I will do what I can, my dearest Mary," George continued, "but Shelley is headstrong."

I lifted my head. He smiled the smile he had first bestowed upon me when he had jumped out of another boat, on another shore, so long ago. It was the smile of a grown-up in a world of juveniles. I offered my hand, and he kissed it. Then, remembering I was not decently clad, I gathered the shawl closer around my nightdress. "But now, George, you must come up to the house."

The kitchen was very dark after the brilliant light outside. As George and I entered we almost collided with a newly-awakened Shelley. Struggling excitedly into his waistcoat, he greeted George. "Is she fitted and ready? Is there wind enough for us to cast off?"

"Of course." George sat down and cut himself some bread. "After I have breakfasted."

With little regard for Percy, who was playing on the floor with a wooden mouse on wheels, Shelley strode out of the kitchen door and ran down the beach. We saw him hopping and splashing in the water. Then he stopped, turned to grin at us, turned back, almost overbalanced, and whooped with glee at the sight of the boat. Even Milly, who was usually overawed by George's presence, laughed.

"Edward! Edward!" Shelley cupped his hands around his mouth and called up at the windows of the villa. "Edward! The boat is come!"

George was sitting contentedly at the table, eating bread and cheese. "A toy, I believe you said?"

I picked up my little boy and sat down, signalling to Milly to bring a pitcher of wine. "Do not stay away long, George," I begged. "I want Shelley here with me. I do not feel well, and do not want to be left alone with Jane and the children. I have been left often before, but never in such a place as this."

George did not speak, but pressed my shoulder.

When Edward and Jane appeared, George took them to admire the boat, leaving me with Percy on my lap and a heart full of longing. Longing for what, I knew not. For my lost children. For my husband's elusive love. For something I could not name.

Percy squirmed, resisting my arms with all his strength – he wanted to go and see the boat too. I put him down, and he ran out to join them, jumping into Shelley's arms. I put on an old petticoat and joined them barefoot. Shelley did not kiss me.

Within half an hour the three men had boarded the boat and cast off, and were clambering about telling each other what to do, and laughing and pretending to push one another into the water.

"Stay close by the shore!" I called.

"Do as the boy tells you!" instructed Jane.

But the wind had already taken the sails, and they were too far away to hear.

Monster

I never saw sea more beautiful than the waters of the bay at Lerici. Its colours were the deepest blue and purple, changing with the current and the weather. At twilight, when the lights on the fishing boats bobbed like fireflies in the bluish air, the sheen on the water was smoother than glass.

Beyond the reach of the bay the grey mist of storms might obscure the horizon, but Lerici was sheltered from the winds by the headland. The sea was so calm that any reflection – the village, the masts of the moored boats, the rising moon – was a perfect representation of itself. Jane and I never tired of walking with Milly and the children in the shade of the olive grove that lay behind the villa, watching the metallic solidity of the water under the Italian sky.

Edward and Shelley sailed their new toy round the headland with George, then George went back to Livorno, where he kept the *Bolivar*. While he was away they spent each day out on the sea, coming back with faces as leather-brown as any fisherman's and appetites greater than our housekeeping funds could satisfy.

We also received a visit from Claire. There was no doubt that grief and experience had changed her. Her pertness had become cynicism; the outlines of her face were harder. She was losing the pliable prettiness that had been the scourge of my happiness for so long.

But prolonged separation and the loss of our children had nevertheless united us: I could not be harder on my sister than life itself had been. And on an airless June afternoon, fate decreed that once again she and I would face elemental forces together.

I felt unwell. I had not been strong since Percy's birth, and this weakness, in addition to our double bereavement and the cold chasm between Shelley and me, had made me ill. Jane and I were both worn out by the daily challenge of putting food on the table and keeping ourselves and our children clean in this most primitive corner of Italy. My body could not support the life of the child I carried. That desperate afternoon, knowing I was bleeding, I collapsed on the kitchen floor.

It is the blood that I remember best. All else is a blur of frantic voices and distorted faces, but I still see the cloths abandoned on the floor, caked crimson, then, as the blood dried, brownish-black.

They could not stop the bleeding. Jane and Claire did their best for a long time, then Claire went in despair for Shelley. "She is dying," I heard her say. "For God's sake, why does the physician not come?"

"He cannot get to this place easily, any more than anyone else can," Shelley told her bleakly. "I have sent for him. Now we must wait."

"But by the time he arrives, Mary will…"

"Quiet! Let me see her."

In that woman's world Shelley did not flinch from acting like a man. He brought ice from the store beneath the house and crushed it with an ice pick. Again and again, his clothes soaked with water and blood, he scooped up crushed ice and applied it.

All I knew was pain. I struggled against unconsciousness, while Jane, weeping the whole time, held my head and Claire bathed my face. I screamed. I could not bear it, but I had to bear it; I knew my child was lost. I must scream – or die.

Later, when the bleeding had at last abated and Jane had gone to Edward, who had waited all those long hours in the kitchen with his head in his hands, Shelley sat down beside my bed. Claire, sniffing, left the room. The physician had sent word that he would come by four in the afternoon; it was now eleven o'clock at night.

"Lie as still as you can," Shelley instructed me – unnecessarily, for I could not move. "You must not start bleeding again. Claire will look after you."

There was only one candle alight. I opened my eyes, and my heart jolted.

"Oh! Oh, God!" I cried aloud.

For I beheld my monster. In the fast-dying candlelight, I encountered for one ghastly minute the hellish vision of my imagination.

Matted hair, drenched and bloody, plastered itself to the creature's cheeks. He wore a filthy shirt, smeared with gore. Dark-circled, luminous eyes gazed in exhaustion from their bony sockets. The countenance, whose flesh stretched over bones as clear as a naked skull, was sunken, and glistened in the meagre light. The pallor of the face was alabaster-white, alabaster-smooth, and regarded me with the frozen gaze of a statue.

"Shelley!" I screamed. "Shelley, where are you?"

"Calm yourself, Mary," came his familiar voice from behind the dreadful mask he wore. "I am here."

"I thought –" My lips were dry. "I thought you were –"

"I am here," he repeated, stroking my hand. "Do not be afraid."

It was almost dark. Shelley took another candle and lit it from the one that was almost spent. I watched him perform this simple domestic task, my gaze following his white hands, my heart filled to bursting.

"Did you save my life?" I asked.

He leant near me. Like Claire, he had lost his angelic beauty. But he remained my angel and my monster; I could not escape.

"I did what any husband would do," he said softly. "And you would do the same for me, if my life was in danger. Now, go to sleep until the doctor arrives."

When he had gone, I wept. For what he had said, but much more for what he had *not*. Why, *why* did he keep his love hovering tantalizingly close, but always further away than I could reach?

I recovered slowly. After Claire had gone, I settled down to long days of convalescence. Jane would not let me help her or Milly. I sat on the beach or the rocks, watching as Edward and Shelley amused themselves "improving" the *Don Juan*.

As usual, Shelley could not resist flattering George by imitation. Within a week of George's visit to Lerici aboard the large, impressive *Bolivar*, my husband had summoned the boat-builder Roberts. New, higher masts had appeared on the *Don Juan*, and narrow decking had been placed each side of its cabin.

"Whatever are they doing?" Jane wondered, shading her eyes against the sun. "Do they need to scamper about like rats, merely to get a boat fitted up?" She looked at me in exasperation. "You do not think they mean to *race* Lord Byron's boat, do you, Mary?"

"Would such an idea surprise you?"

"Not at all. And they would surely lose, whatever improvements they made!"

She sighed, and then laughed. I laughed too. A swell of relief surged through me: I had survived, and Percy was thriving, and Italy was glorious, despite all its local hardships. Life would, as always, go on.

That evening Shelley made an announcement. "Edward and I have a most excellent plan," he said.

"Oh no, not another *plan*!" said Jane good-humouredly.

"Yes, indeed," insisted Shelley. "Edward and I set off tomorrow to sail the *Don Juan* to Livorno, to see George."

"Alone?" asked Jane, widening her eyes. "But are you sure −"

"Not quite alone," interrupted Edward. "George's boy will accompany us, remember."

"Thank the Lord," said Jane mildly, exchanging a look with me.

George's boy, whose name we had discovered to be Charles, was at that moment eating soup with Milly in the kitchen. As a necessary addition to our household he had to be fed, and Milly, only a couple of years older, was not averse to his company.

"We leave tomorrow," said Shelley enthusiastically, "and return one week from that day. At least, that is our plan."

"Ah! The plan!" laughed Jane.

The next day was a blazing, shimmering July day. The water in the bay looked as purple as Caesar's robes, but according to Edward there was enough breeze to allow a voyage to Livorno. We watched them stack their belongings on the boat. With her feet bare and her dark hair gleaming in the glare of the morning, Jane looked as lovely as a Greek statue magically given movement and colour. The children were almost as excited as their fathers; they shrieked as they played in the spray, wet to the skin but happy as savages.

The *Don Juan* lay at her moorings, looking every inch as romantic as Shelley could desire. His belief that the sea is in every Englishman's blood was about to receive its strictest test, but that morning even my jaded eye was seduced by the beauty of the boat.

Her white masts caught the sparkle of the sunlight as the boy climbed up to the yard-arm and began untying the ropes. The sight of the mainsail dropping like the veil of a giant's bride stirred my soul. It was a small boat, according to Shelley, and in no way as gorgeous as the *Bolivar*, of which he would remain forever envious. But to me it looked large, fearsome, powerful.

I put on my bonnet and followed Jane to the water's edge. Half my heart dreaded this adventure. But the other half was jealous of the easy, masculine world that allowed it. I had not often wished to be a man, except during child-birth, but I wished it now. I wanted to share with Shelley what he was sharing with Edward.

For shame, I said to myself, watching Edward embrace Jane. *Are you so weary of being jealous of a woman that you welcome the chance to be jealous of a man?*

Shelley was already on the boat. He had taken a curt leave of me in the house, saying he did not care for displays of affection in front of servants, and was now assisting the boy with the sails. I watched him, thinking how mysterious it was that this tall, bony, untidily groomed man, now almost thirty years old and bound to me by the ties of marriage, was now bound to the world by fame and reputation.

The impulsive early career of the aristocratic atheist Shelley had been was no longer discussed in literary circles. Shelley's poetry was now acknowledged by critics and public as masterful, and it was ever a source of pain to me that the success of his poetic output of the past few years seemed to have eased neither his nightmares nor his desire to punish his health by means of his restrictive diet, and of course alcohol and opium. But any mention I made of this was met with the observation that sales of all his published poetry together had never remotely matched those of even *one* of George's best-loved works.

"Even *Adonais*, my lament for poor Keats," he would say peevishly, "a poem I consider to be among my finest, did not sell better than George's *Don Juan*." Then, with a sigh, "George must have the common touch, which I lack."

Despite his pessimism, however, Shelley's increasing fame as a poet was eclipsing his notoriety. Gossips had less to gossip about now that we had been married for several years. Claire had left our household and her child of dubious paternity was dead. Indeed, we had been away from England for so many years, and were now in such a lonely place, that our unconventional lifestyle was invisible. Perhaps it was even forgotten.

Shelley called to me from the deck. I waved, and called back, and they began to haul in the anchor. There were tears in my eyes. He was still my unholy angel, however much the years had changed him and made him famous, and I was still drowning in love. It was not lack of love that had maintained the frozen waste between us for so many months, but fear.

Shelley had turned from me because I could not love him as I wished, for fear of his not returning my love. That precious moment after he saved me from death had dissolved into bitterness when he had merely told me that I would have done the same for him. He had not saved me because he loved me.

Long after that day I wondered why I did not do what instinct beckoned me to. As the boat pulled away from the shore, and the wind began to make Shelley's hair whip this way and that and his clothes shudder against his limbs, longing surged through my body, and overcame me. I wanted to run into the water and, while he was still within earshot, tell him how dear he was to me. I wanted to tell him that I did not think he had murdered our children, or betrayed Harriet, or desired any woman but me.

But I did not do it. I ran two or three steps towards the water, but Jane, knowing how weak I had been since my blood loss, caught me and lowered me gently to the sand. She put her arms around me and let me weep, until Percy came to see what was the matter with his mother and the boat disappeared around the headland.

The Burnt-out Heart

In Italy there are laws relating to death which might seem strict, even violent, to inhabitants of a more northern climate. Shelley once told me that after John Keats had died of consumption, everything in his apartment in Rome had to be burned, for fear of infection. But in England doctors do not believe consumption to be infectious. Doctors and lawyers! What a weighty influence they have on all our lives, and deaths!

This law is strict, but there is another even stricter. To avoid plague being brought to Italy, the quarantine law states that anything washed up by the sea onto the coast – even a human body – must be burned.

Before Shelley, Edward and the boy set off for Livorno, I barely knew of this law. But within two weeks its existence had assumed a bewildering importance.

A week after their arrival in Livorno, the crew of the *Don Juan* set out for their return voyage to Lerici, in weather quite different from the brilliant calm in which they had left us. Away from the shelter of the coast, a sudden squall blew up, and the *Don Juan* sailed into it.

But the hull of the boat was not designed to support the top-heavy mast Shelley had insisted be added. When a violent gust caught the inexperienced sailors unawares, the vessel quickly overturned and her passengers were thrown into the treacherous waters almost before they knew what had happened.

This was the only comfort anyone could offer Jane and me. Poor Edward, accustomed as he was to large vessels, could not have predicted or remedied the fate of a small boat at the mercy of the weather. Roberts himself, who was watching the *Don Juan* through a telescope from the Livorno lighthouse, saw the storm envelop several larger vessels as well as Shelley's boat. When it had passed, he again looked through the telescope. All the other boats were there, but, as the last drops of mist evaporated, he realized that the craft he had built had disappeared.

The horror of those days refuses to fade. It is as bright in my memory as heaven itself, or the deranged alchemist's dream of gold.

Jane and I travelled to Livorno to try and find out what had happened. We returned to Lerici without news, but the dreadful truth awaited us there. A letter from Roberts said that three bodies had been washed up on the beach at Livorno, and, according to Italian law, had been buried there immediately. Within days they would have to be burned.

Jane diminished before my eyes. With her beauty concealed by the blank face of shock, she sank noiselessly to the floor, her dress mushrooming around her. "Is it certain, Mary?" she whispered.

"We shall hear soon enough," I said.

I left her and went to my bedroom. I lay on the bed, exhausted, until I heard a carriage, and Milly crying. It was Edward's friend Trelawny, a man I had never properly trusted and whose presence in my life was dictated solely by the whim of a husband I was now almost sure I would never see again. But I was grateful to him for making the difficult journey. To receive confirmation of my widowhood by letter would have been insupportable.

I went to receive him. "Thank you for coming," I said, as he bowed.

He could tell by my face that I needed no protection from the truth. "They are identified," he said. "Where is Mrs Williams?"

"Let her rest. She has not slept these twenty hours. I shall tell her."

He bowed again. Poor Trelawny: he was an ineffectual person thrust onto the pages of history by dint of his acquaintance with a famous poet. Even as I looked at him I wondered if that fate would also be mine. But how dearly I wanted to secure my place in history by my own hand!

"After so long in the water, and in such stormy weather, the bodies were battered beyond recognition," he said. He did not look at me. Dear God, he could not.

"How was the identification made?" I asked faintly. "And who made it?"

He still could not look at me. He lowered his chin. The large stock he wore at his throat muffled his voice. "Roberts identified Edward by his boots. The boy was the most whole. I myself saw the corpse of your husband, Mrs Shelley."

I waited in horror.

"It was very far gone, very far gone indeed. But his jacket remained, and although I did not recognize the jacket itself, in the pocket I found a book I knew definitely to be Shelley's."

Trelawny did not give in to weeping, though I feared he was close to it. From his pack he brought an object almost unrecognizable as a book, and presented it to me. "It contains his writing on the flyleaf. It is still readable. The Italian authorities accepted this identification, and I rescued it before they threw him into a makeshift grave. My dear Mrs Shelley, how sorry I am to have to bring you this!"

I shrank back, holding onto the back of a chair for support. I knew which book Shelley habitually carried in his pocket: the volume of Keats's poems from my father's bookshop. It was the voice of Adonais. I had copied out *Adonais* many times, but since Shelley's death the prophetic nature of the poem's closing lines had not struck me. Now, they came back to me with force:

> "My spirit's bark is driven,
> Far from the shore, far from the trembling throng
> Whose sails were never to the tempest given;
> The massy earth and sphered skies are riven!
> I am borne darkly, fearfully, afar;
> Whilst, burning through the inmost veil of Heaven,
> The soul of Adonais, like a star,
> Beacons from the abode where the Eternal are."

Trembling, I took the misshapen book. "Thank you, Mr Trelawny, for your pains," I said, gesturing for him to sit down. "You will eat and drink with us, will you not?"

I had Milly bring wine, bread and cheese, and Trelawny talked for a long time. Jane awoke and joined us, and although we wept, I knew that our ordeal, like Shelley's, was almost over. We could not attend the burning of the bodies but awaited Trelawny's account of it on his return.

Each minute of the next three days is distilled, second by second, in my heart. Jane and I lived in a dream, attending to the children and helping Milly by laying and clearing the table, baking, washing clothes and hanging them out to dry. We wandered in the garden, on the beach and in the olive grove, clinging to each other.

The weather was hot and still. The sky and the sea were one, a dome of deepest blue, the horizon barely visible. Though we were aware that only a few miles along the coast a fire had consumed the bodies of the two men we had loved, eloped with, borne children for, we did not speak of it. We wrote no letters, we made no arrangements. The world rolled on, but we did not notice it.

On the fourth day Trelawny broke the spell. He arrived by boat, carried over a calm sea by an experienced crew. As he stepped out clumsily, wiping his forehead with his handkerchief, I could not help but torture myself. What unforgiving God, I wondered, had made the sea calm today, yet less than a week ago had sent a storm to drown my husband? Had Shelley been right all along when he said that God does not hear our prayers because there *is* no God?

We took Trelawny to the house, where he described how he and Roberts had laid the bodies on metal racks, and watched while the fire blackened them.

"Write it, Mr Trelawny!" urged Jane, her small hands

covering her cheeks, her eyes bright. "Write it down, so that the scene will be recorded for future generations!"

"Should I?" Trelawny turned to me uneasily. "Is not a personal tragedy best kept private?"

I swallowed. "Mr Trelawny, it *is* a personal tragedy for Mrs Williams. But for me it is not. Mrs Williams is right: the events of Shelley's death should be reported to the world. Those who have made him famous deserve to know the circumstances of his end."

"Very well, then." He contemplated the floor for a moment, then he raised his eyes to meet mine. "May I see you alone for a few minutes, Mrs Shelley?"

"Of course."

I led him into the garden. We had not gone two steps down the path when he stopped and withdrew something from the pocket of his jacket. He offered it to me. "Please, Mrs Shelley, take this. I retrieved it from the embers."

I thought it would be Shelley's watch, or a piece of his clothing. But when I unwrapped the object from its covering of filthy, blackened paper, shock made me gasp. I almost threw the thing to the ground: it was Shelley's heart.

"The fire had almost destroyed it," explained Trelawny, much agitated. "As you see, it is black and burnt out. But I give you my word that this is the heart of your dear husband, snatched from his funeral pyre." He took out his handkerchief again and wiped his face. "It was the least I could do. Of Edward Williams nothing remained."

Revulsion and joy fought each other as I made my reply. I thanked him, and we gazed together at the small, charred thing in my hand. Then I wrapped it again, and put it in the pocket of my dress, and went with him back into the house.

I do not think to this day that he had any idea of the over-whelming import of his gift.

For eight years I had fought for the very thing that now lay in my pocket. At last, by the cruellest means possible, I was in possession of Shelley's heart.

Later that evening, when Trelawny had departed and Jane was in bed, I went to the trunk in my bedroom, which contained my secret manuscript. There it lay, under my winter gowns. I took it, and, holding it close to my breast, returned downstairs to the drawing-room. I sat at the writing-desk, placed the manuscript on it and felt in the pocket of my dress for Trelawny's gift.

I unwrapped the paper and looked at the heart. I remembered how repulsive Shelley had found the notion of cutting up body parts for experiments. How he had shrieked with fear that night at the Villa Diodati when the idea for this very manuscript had been born!

I tore some clean paper from the back of my manuscript. Nausea rose in my throat, but I wrapped the heart anew, making a tighter, neater package than Trelawny's. I felt a strong desire never to look at it again. Knowing it was mine was enough; I did not need to display it to the world.

The story was nearly finished. Proudly I took a pen and sharpened it. The dream was over: all that remained of Shelley was his ashes, and the thing contained in the package that lay beside me on the table. He was neither my angel nor my monster any more. The unbearable sorrow we had endured, the passion we had felt and the estrangement we had not been able to conquer had vanished from the world. I was alone now.

But I was not lonely. I opened the manuscript; the black

words on the title page presented themselves boldly on the white paper. As I read them, my heart folded with love – for the man I had lost and the man I had made.

Frankenstein,
or The Modern Prometheus,

I read. Then I dipped my pen in the ink and added,

by Mary Shelley.

"Don't cry. We won't be parted, I promise."

It is 1662 and England is reeling from the after-effects of civil war, with its clashes of faith and culture.

Seventeen-year-old Will returns home after completing his studies, to begin an apprenticeship arranged by his wealthy father. Susanna, a young Quaker girl, leaves her family to become a servant in the same town.

Theirs is a story that speaks across the centuries, telling of love and the struggle to stay true to what is most important – despite parents, society and even the law.

But is the love between Will and Susanna strong enough to survive – no matter what?

ANN TURNBULL

When her grandfather dies, Tamar inherits a box containing a series of clues and coded messages.

Out of the past, another Tamar emerges, a man involved in the terrifying world of resistance fighters in Nazi-occupied Holland half a century earlier. His story is one of passionate love, jealousy and tragedy set against the daily fear and casual horror of the Second World War. Unravelling it will transform the younger Tamar's life.